RESISTING DARKNESS

AMY L. GALE

RESISTING DARKNESS
BY: AMY L. GALE

Title © 2017 Amy L Gale

Copyright notice: All rights reserved under the International and Pan-American Copyright Conventions. No part of this book may be reproduced or transmitted in any form or by any means, electronic or mechanical, including photocopying, recording, or by any information storage and retrieval system, without permission in writing from the publisher.

This is a work of fiction. Names, places, characters and incidents are either the product of the author's imagination or are used fictitiously, and any resemblance to any actual persons, living or dead, organizations, events or locales is entirely coincidental.

Warning: the unauthorized reproduction or distribution of this copyrighted work is illegal. Criminal copyright infringement, including infringement without monetary gain, is investigated by the FBI and is punishable by up to 5 years in prison and a fine of $250,000.

Resisting Darkness
How can you destroy the world's monsters when you're in love with one?

Supernatural hunter, Dex Jager, will stop at nothing to find the vampire brood that captured his sister, and take them down one by one. After a motorcycle accident lands him in the small town of Whispering Pines, he finds himself in the middle of a murder investigation and partnered with Cora Fisher, the beautiful town coroner. As Dex and Cora grow closer and secrets surface, Dex is faced with the toughest decision of his life. How can you resist the darkness when it's the one thing you love?

1

STRANDED

"Hey. Anybody there?" I pry my eyes open catching glimpses of chrome scattered along the pavement. The stench of burning rubber rips through the air. Darkness swallows the last hints of sunlight, leaving the road abandoned. Son of a bitch, I laid down the Harley...again. I rub my throbbing temples, trying to get my bearings straight. The last thirty seconds rush through my mind like a freight train. Goddammit, the bloodsucker got away...or maybe not. I try to pull myself up but hellfire burns through my arm. I lie flat against the pavement, unable to will myself to rise. Long auburn hair flashes through my field of vision followed by a high-pitched growl. Everything goes dark.

"Dex...can you hear me?" A muffled voice, sweet as honey, rings through my ears.

Did I get lucky? Jesus Christ...not with one of them. I gasp and pop open my eyes. A perfect face hovers over mine. Flawless skin, auburn hair any mermaid would kill for, and a body hotter than the flames of the ninth level of hell. Am I dead? She's got to be an angel.

I flash a shit-eating grin a split second before my mind goes into overdrive. Hell, she's one of them. I spring from the bed, running my hands along my neck to check for bite marks. The blue gown draped around me falls open in the back, showing off more than I usually do in the first couple of minutes I meet a girl, barring a few exceptions.

I fling my hands back and wrap the gown around me. These heinous contraptions only exist in one place on earth. I glance around the small hospital room. Sunlight shines in through the large window illuminating a variety of equipment hooked up to my body. Wait, it's daylight; she can't be one of them.

She holds up her hands and walks toward me. "I guess you don't remember what went down."

If it was her, I had one hell of a night. I stare at her honey-brown eyes. They suck me in to the depths of her soul. Something about her, she's...different. I mean, yeah she's hot as a three-alarm fire and way sexier than most girls I see when I wake up in a hospital but that's not it. I run my hands through my hair. No more thinking, not until this vice grip loosens its hold on my brain.

I shrug. "I crashed my hog. Other than that, I've got no clue." Doubt she'd believe me if I told her I was chasing a vampire so I could beat the truth out of him and find out where they took my sister.

"I'm Cora." She holds out her hand.

I loosen the grip on my robe and shake hers. "There's no way I'd forget you." Okay, not my best line but this time it's the truth.

"I'm the coroner of Whispering Pines. I drove by and saw the wreck. I brought you here and figured I'd stick around. You know...in case I got called." She flashes a quick smile. "I had to check your wallet for ID. Are you in town for work?"

If someone goes through your wallet they already know the answer to that question. She's got no clue how much 'work' I'm here to handle. "Yeah." I sit back down on the bed and rip the IV out of my hand. "Easier to do if I had some clothes."

She squirms, like my blood is going to give her hepatitis from the mere sight. She bends down and pulls my duffle bag from underneath a chair. "Interesting equipment for a Fish and Wildlife Officer." She looks me up and down and tosses the bag on the bed.

Goddammit. How am I supposed to explain this? My heart pounds. Is it from her questioning or the way she catches her lip between her teeth?

"I collect artifacts." Some of the shit in that bag is older than God. I rummage through, looking for a t-shirt and any pair of underwear. Okay, so dead man's blood, a silver dagger, and a homemade stake aren't things you'd see in the Smithsonian.

"Uh-huh." Her eyes widen as I pull my jeans out of the bag. A red hue creeps over her cheeks. She spins around at warp speed.

Does Miss hot-as-fuck coroner want to give me a thorough exam? Hell, I'm game. I bet she can raise the dead with one touch. She sure as hell made me stand at attention.

A short woman in her mid-forties with a mop of blonde hair piled on top of her head, wearing a white coat at least two sizes too big, marches through the door and quickly closes the curtain. "Mr. Jager. How are we feeling today?"

"Ready to jet." I pull on my socks and slip into my sneakers. "Any news about my bike?" Dear God, please let them take good care of my baby.

"It'll be a few days until the necessary repairs are finished. I went ahead and phoned the Overbrook Hotel for you. I can't discharge you with no transportation and nowhere to stay, Mr. Jager."

So I'm stuck in bumble-fuck wherever the hell I am for a few days. What are the chances the coroner finds me on the most desolate road in town? Maybe there's more to this girl than brains-like-Einstein and a hot piece of ass. Looks like I'll be working with Cora until I can trace the murders in this town to the bloodsuckers. Who knows? Maybe I'll destroy a few of them in the process.

"Thanks, doc." I slide on my leather jacket just as the doctor leaves the room. She does a double take, and then quickly scurries away. Aha, they should market this coat as the panty dropper. It's gotten me lucky more times than I can count.

Cora hands me two silver bullets that must've fallen out of my bag. "Guess you'll need these for your...investigation?"

"Never know." I sling the bag around a shoulder. I've read the headlines. Hell, it's why I'm here. Two bodies found in the woods, completely drained of their blood. Unless a leech came in contact with some type of radioactive substance causing it become a giant, no animal in existence is responsible for this type of attack. "Never hurts to be prepared." I wink. Jesus, she probably thinks I'm some psychotic killer infringing on her town I've got to play it cool before she has me committed.

She takes a step back, fidgeting with her fingers. "Come on, I'll walk you out."

What's with her? Last time a girl acted like this in front of me she ended up stealing my wallet the morning after a one-nighter. Sure, I can make a girl's panties bunch but not like this. The sun shines through the window, illuminating gold highlights in her hair. If she was a bloodsucker she'd be burned to a crisp by now. I'm pretty sure she's not after my cash. What's the deal?

I brush against her as I pass; her perfume radiates a meadow of flowers through the small room. I inhale deeply, trying to breathe in her essence. She stands still, almost like she's playing dead so I don't notice her. Honey, a blind man can see the white-hot sex coming from every pore of that body.

She follows, like she's afraid I'm going to pounce on her if she lowers her guard. I get it; the stuff in my bag probably freaked her out. I'll just tell her I'm a dungeons and dragons master and very enthusiastic about my title. Maybe I should start out in her comfort zone, with some questions about the case.

"Any leads so far?" I slow down and walk beside her through the stench of bleach filling the hospital hallway.

She shifts to the right, almost walking into the white wall as a doctor passes. "The sheriff and I are checking out some prints in the mud near the scene of the last victim." She moves as far from me as possible once the hallway clears.

What the hell? I bend my head down and do a quick pit-sniff check. Nope, still smells like that cheap deodorant I got at the last gas station. I lean against the wall near the elevator and push the button. She nibbles her lip and stares at the doors as they slowly open.

"Ladies first." I wink and stand behind her. Damn, the rear view is just and good. Black heels, dark jeans hugging every curve on her body, and a black shirt hanging off her shoulders just enough to attract any vampire in a fifty-mile radius. Maybe I need to stick around her...really close.

She steps inside the elevator as soon as the doors open enough to clear her body. Jesus, she's like an animal trapped in a cage. She takes a deep breath and leans against the back corner.

"I hate elevators." I stand beside her and watch the doors close. I get it; no one likes being stuck in a tin box that could drop at any second. Maybe if she thinks we're in this together she'll relax. Misery loves company, right?

She nods and nibbles her lip like she's about to chew it off. A droplet of sweat runs down her hairline. Jesus, is she okay? I drop my duffle bag onto the floor and move toward her. Her face turns ashen like a porcelain doll.

I run my hand along her cheek. "Should I press the button and take you back up?"

She closes her eyes and swallows hard. "I'm fine. Just need to get away from here."

Wait, isn't a coroner at the hospital all the time...especially the morgue? "Interesting job choice for someone with a fear of hospitals."

She pops open her eyes, shooting daggers at me. "It's not the hospital I need to get away from." She steps forward, pushing me out of the way and stands in front of the doors, arms folded across her chest.

I hold up my hands. "Whoa, what's got your panties all in a bunch?"

She glares at me over her shoulder. "You have absolutely no effect on my panties." She fidgets with her fingers and turns back around.

Let's see if that's even remotely true. I lean forward and press the elevator emergency stop button. Something more than a fear of elevators or hospitals is going down in her head and I need answers.

She swings around toward me but I block access to the buttons. "Are you insane? You can't stop an elevator in a hospital. You're putting lives at risk, you asshole." Her face burns crimson.

"How about you tell me what the hell is going on here?" She has to be involved in this somehow. If she's protecting one of those bloodsuckers then she's just as bad as them.

"I'm trying to get out of here and back to work on the case but I'm stuck babysitting you." Her hands ball into fists. "If I knew you'd be this much trouble I would've left you in the road to fend for yourself against—" She stops dead. Her eyes widen.

"Against what?" Go ahead...say it. She knows exactly what's happening in this town. I get it. She wants me out...but why?

She drops her arms and breathes deep. "Whatever animal is doing this."

Animal...more like monster. Okay, so she pretty much saved my life. I guess I owe her at the least an apology. I run a hand through my hair and blow air out my cheeks. "Thank you...for picking me up."

She nods. "You're welcome."

"Can we start over?" I hold out my hand. "I'm Dex Jager and I'm indebted to you for rescuing me." Chicks love lines like that one.

She flashes a quick half-smile. "I'm Cora Fisher and you're the first person I found on the side of the road still alive."

I let out a slight laugh. She got me there. In her line of work the dead don't normally argue with her...as far as I know. Maybe that's her whole deal—not a people person.

I press the run button. The elevator jolts like the hand of God grabbed it. Cora stumbles, holding out her arms to steady herself. No such luck. She smacks into me full force. Maybe divine intervention is on my side, or something else is going down here. I wrap my arms around her waist and hold her against me, burying my face in her hair. I breathe deep, taking in the sweet scent of honey mixed with her fruity perfume. I tighten my grip like she's going to run out of my life the second she gets the chance. I can't let her go.

The bell chimes, resonating through the small space. She squirms, wiggling herself out of my death grip as the doors open to the lobby. I drop my arms to my sides and stare into her light-brown eyes, light like melted caramel and just as warm.

She pats down her shirt and steps onto the tile foyer. "Well, I'm glad you're okay." She digs in her purse and pulls out a business card. "If you need anything while you're here investigating the animal attacks, give my office a call."

I follow her like a lost puppy. "Will do."

Her ass sways side to side as she walks away. Her heels click against the tile, almost in time with my racing heart. I'm suffocating, caught in the depths of her being. What the fuck is happening to me?

She picks up the pace when she reaches the glass doors and heads to the parking garage like a rabid wolverine is on her tail. Maybe this is her whole hard-to-get routine. I mean, I've been with more chicks than I can count. A lot of them hotter than the flames of hell, but Cora, well she's a whole new breed of woman. One I've never encountered before and can't seem to resist. Maybe that's how Ruby felt. Jesus, what am I thinking?

The minute she steps outside I take a deep breath, clearing my fuzzy mind. Did I hit my head harder than I thought in the wreck? What the hell is wrong with me? Love 'em and leave 'em, that's my motto. Hell, I'm never in one place long enough for more than that anyway. Maybe she gets it. Yeah, that's probably it; she wants to stay as far away as possible so she doesn't get sucked in by my charm.

I wipe my sweaty palms along my jeans and sling my duffle bag over a shoulder. Come on Dex, focus. You're here to catch the bloodsucker doing this, not chase tail. God knows what they've done to Ruby, or if she's human, let alone my sister anymore.

I trek outside to the parking garage. Shit. No wheels and no friggin' clue where the Overbrook Hotel is in this town. Do they even have Uber way up here in the sticks?

A black BMW pulls up to the stop sign by the exit blasting "Strutter" by KISS. Jesus Christ, someone in this town actually listens to good music. The car stays parked there for at least thirty seconds. Guess they're either gawking at the only person in town they don't know or ready call the cops on me for loitering. If the small town folks are as friendly as their reputation, maybe I can at least get some directions.

I wave in a "hey I promise I'm not going to kill you" sort of way and walk over to the shiny black car. Tinted windows, dual exhaust, whoever's in here wants to go unnoticed and be able to make a quick getaway. Sounds kind of familiar.

I lean over as the window slowly descends. "Hey, any idea where the Overbrook—" The fruity scent hits me like a freight train. My heart beats into overdrive.

Cora turns down the music. "On the other side of town." She taps her fingers on the steering wheel and cringes like an eternal struggle is going down in her brain. "Want a ride?"

"Yeah." I trot to the passenger side and hop in like a rabbit on caffeine. Way to play it cool, Dex. I close the door and toss my duffle bag on the floor. "Thanks."

She stares down at the black tattered bag for a few seconds and then back up at me. "Seatbelt." She points toward the strangling harness I never wear. "I don't feel like coming back here to identify your body if something happens." She nibbles her lip.

Oh, something is definitely happening here. "You're the boss."

She flashes a quick smile and takes off down the road. I turn up the radio and lean back in my seat, trying to restrain myself from pulling her into the back and giving her the ride of her life.

Jesus, for some God-knows-why reason I can barely control myself. Cora consumes every thought in my brain. Is the hunter inside me coming out full force or am I falling victim to something else?

2

SECRETS

"So this is where the magic happens." I stroll into Cora's office like I I'm ready to set up a cubicle and make a residence for myself.

"Can I help you?" she says in a professional voice. Her auburn hair falls in perfect loose waves along the outline of her porcelain skin. She taps a pen on her lip with a trembling hand.

"Yeah. Came here to join the KISS army." I shift my gaze to the radio on her desk blasting "Detroit Rock City". Hot as fire with kick-ass taste in music. Where the hell has this girl been hiding all my life?

She grabs the dial and turns it down like she's a teenager and her mom just burst into her bedroom. "It helps me work."

I nod. "Zeppelin helps me." I stroll through her quaint office, staring at wooden desk that could be mistaken for an antique, and the wooden walls, no doubt built sometime in the seventies. A small table with two chairs placed at the back end of the room makes it look more like a waiting room than a coroner's office. What gives?

"Um, Mr. Jager. Didn't think I'd see you so soon. Did you

need my assistance with something?" She closes the folder on her desk and looks up at me with a concerned stare.

Yeah, with more than even I can comprehend at the moment. "What's with the Mr. Jager? Don't you think you could call me Dex? I mean, you saw me half naked."

Her face turns crimson. Maybe she likes what she saw a little too much. She raises her eyebrows and gives me that you've-got-to-be-kidding me look. "I thought it be better to be professional."

I muffle a smile. "I wanted to see your files on the animal attacks. See if we can come up with a theory." I slide my hands in my pockets and walk to her desk. "You've been following this case from the beginning. Thought maybe we'd put our heads together." Believe me, there's nothing I want more than putting our body parts together.

"I normally work alone." She shuffles through a few files on her desk. "But the quicker we get this solved the better." She nibbles her lip. "You know...to protect the town."

Why do I get the feeling she's protecting more than the town? She rolls her chair backward and stands, passing a folder to me the same way you'd throw meat at a lion—fast and from as far away as possible.

I plop down in the hard wooden chair at the front of her desk and scoot it next to her. "Looks like it's a change for both of us then." I breathe deep taking in the sweet nectar of her skin.

She clears her throat like she's suffocating from my presence. Why is she so repulsed by me? It's the notorious Catch-22, I want her more than ever and she can't stand the sight of me. New goal, change that in a hurry. Or show her exactly what she could have if she plays her cards right. Could she be doing the whole hard-to-get deal?

She takes the folder from my hand and flips it open to the second page. "Here's the first victim. Female, traveling through town." She flips to another page. "Body found near the base of a tree, drained of ninety percent of her blood.

"We?" I lean in closer; my breath blows strands of her hair against her face.

Her hand trembles as she reaches for a picture inside the file. "Sheriff Townsend and I." She takes a deep breath, slowly exhaling.

Ah, I get it. She has a thing going with the sheriff. "Are you guys working on this case really close together?" I flash a half smile.

"Excuse me, what are you implying?" She shoots a death stare at me.

I shrug. "Wondering how involved you two are...on the case." Yeah, I get it. It's none of my business who she's fucking. Not yet anyway.

"Well, we're both trying to solve it, just like you." She rolls her eyes and shuffles through the papers. "Are you paying attention to something other than my breasts?"

I jerk my head back. Dammit, caught red-handed. Of course this time I didn't even know I was doing it. She sucks me in like a black hole, into the depths of her being. All right, I'm here for a reason, and unfortunately it's not to bang the hot redhead coroner.

"Okay. Blood drained near the base of a tree. Was it in the woods or out in the open?" Looks like the work of a vampire, probably a brood somewhere around here. If I didn't wreck and got that blood sucker I could've stopped them.

She turns the page to a map. "Right here, pretty deep in Rickett's Forest." She points to a place on the map.

I slide my finger along Route 80 until our skin touches. Tingles rush through my body like an electric shock. "If we travel this road we can get there in about ten minutes."

She pulls her hand away like she just touched a hot stove. "More like a half-hour. The bridge is out."

Great. The blood sucker must have destroyed it to buy some time. Those bastards are smarter than they seem. How the hell did my sister fall for their bullshit? "You up for giving me a tour?"

She taps her fingers on the desk like she's frantically sending an SOS in Morse code. "We'd have to hike from the bridge to the crime scene." She looks me up and down, her eyebrow slightly raised. "Can you even hike in those boots?"

I glance at my black motorcycle boots. "I can do more than you think in these babies." If she just says the word, I'll show her everything I've got.

She huffs. "Come on, tough guy, let's see if you can keep up." She grabs her keys from the desk and takes the folder.

I stare at her tight ass as she slides on the hiking boots she has situated next to a pair of black heels near the far wall. Guess she's always prepared...for anything.

My black duffle bag hits me in the chest. I grab it before it falls to the floor. Great, caught again. She might kill me herself in those deep woods, or maybe she has another agenda. An involuntary smile graces my face at the thought of Cora seducing me in the woods.

"Don't forget your...investigative tools." She pulls open the door, letting the cool breeze douse the fire across my hot cheeks. "And whatever you're thinking...not going to happen." She trots out the door like a cat with a mouse in its mouth.

"Not yet, but I'm just getting started, babe." I walk out of her office and close the door. She totally ignores my comment even though I know she heard me.

We get into her car and she fires up the engine. "I Love it Loud" sounds through the speakers. God, every second I'm into this chick even more. I'm in some serious trouble if we don't solve this case soon. I reach over for the volume button to turn it up.

She slaps my hand away. "Driver picks the music."

I hold my hands in the air. "Your car, your rules."

She shifts into Reverse. "Seatbelt."

I exhale loudly and pull on my seatbelt. "Yes Mom, you plan on taking me on a wild ride or something?"

She turns toward me and smirks. "You have no idea." She turns up the music and floors the gas pedal.

Dear God, I think I'm in love.

"You want me to go first? Check for…animals?" I sling my duffle bag over a shoulder and peer through the thick woods. God knows how many bloodsuckers took up residence here. The least I can do is let her have a head start if we find any.

She hops over a log and navigates through a thick patch of woods like she's a deer. "I've got it. Been living here long enough to handle a walk in the woods, Dex." She slithers through a line of massive pine trees.

The way my name rolls off her tongue sends flames raging through me. I let out a low moan and suppress the image of her screaming "Dex!" in ecstasy. Bridge is out, no one for miles; could she be taking me here for more than the investigation? Yeah, right, she's not a banging in the woods kind of chick as far as I know, and I'm sure as hell not that lucky.

I pick up the pace, almost running to keep up with her. Alright, so she has a point about the boots. I'll never admit it to her, though. I leap across a mound of dry leaves. Can't take any chances. Sometimes these bloodsuckers make traps and I'm not about to be some vamp's snack. Plus, if I'm going to be lying on my back in the middle of the woods I'd at least like

Cora hovering over me. The thought sends shockwaves through me.

I catch a glimpse of red hair swaying in the slight breeze. I grab Cora's wrist right before she moves out of reach. "I get it. You're Dora the Explorer. How about we stay together. It won't kill you hang with me for a few hours."

She stops. "It might." Her eyes sweep me from head to toe, electric shocks follow her gaze. "Fine." She points ahead. "Right over that hill is where the first victim was found."

I pass her and maneuver the little hill like a frog on lily pads. "What are you waiting for?"

A low growl forms in her throat. She folds her arms over her chest and walks through the brush. Her crimson cheeks light up the forest and that sweet smelling perfume makes me want to knock her down and lick every inch of her body. God damn, she's even hotter when she's pissed.

We walk through a clearing that opens to a small meadow. Weird? An open patch in the middle of woods that are so thick you can barely see two feet in front of you.

"Any idea where this came from?" I pace around the area. It's like an alien made a crop circle. "Doesn't look like the work of any animal I know."

She shrugs. "Maybe someone made a camp site." She nibbles her lip and hugs her arms around her chest.

I get the feeling she knows more than she's letting on. I get it, she despises me for some God-only-knows reason but I have to find out what she's holding back.

"Why isn't this roped off?" I walk the section of open woods.

"There's caution tape around the tree up ahead...where we found the body." She rushes through the meadow to a large tree like a hot knife through butter. "Here's where the victim was found."

I bend and run my fingers along the dirt on the base of the

tree. Completely clean, not a sign of a blood drop, or struggle. Either the victim allowed herself to be drained and the vampire didn't spill a drop, or someone went through a lot of trouble to erase all vampire-related evidence from the crime scene.

"Looks pretty clean." I circle the tree, glancing along the rough bark. Leaves rustle, dancing in the breeze. The sweet smell of Cora's perfume flows through the air. "Animals don't usually lick every drop of blood from the dirt." I gaze at a tree limb, the bark almost completely torn off, exposing clean wood. "What's up with this?" I point at the limb.

"The body was hanging from there. Guess something chewed the bark." She fidgets with her fingers before sticking them in her pockets.

"A bloodsucking climbing beaver?" Okay, she's an intelligent girl. She sure as hell knows there's no animal in existence that cleans up every drop of blood and rubs bark completely off of a tree limb to rid the scene of all body fluids. Is she leading me on a wild goose chase?

She shrugs. "Animals are your forte. I just find the cause of death and it was loss of blood due to a bite." She looks down at the leaves, avoiding eye contact.

What game is she playing? "Well, then we've got a problem." Maybe I can shake her up a bit into telling the truth, or at least a part of it.

"What do you mean? It had to be an animal." She lifts her gaze to match mine.

"Maybe." I pace around the tree. "At this point, I'm guessing werewolf who's a crime lord in the mafia. This scene is wiped clean and not by an animal."

She rolls her eyes at the werewolf comment. "Are you saying someone is trying to cover this up?" She paces the length of the tree. "Why would someone fake an animal attack?"

"Exactly." There's a breach in the line somewhere and I've

got to find it. Either Sheriff Townsend or another member of the force is trying damn hard to make this crime scene fit their wild animal theory, or this vamp has friends in high places. Doesn't matter, I'm not leaving until I take down this bloodsucker.

"Do you think someone is trying to protect a cougar or something?" She nibbles on her lip.

I get it; we're going with the whole dingo-ate-my-baby deal. "The way the blood was drained from these victims we're looking for a saber tooth tiger." I rest my hand in the small of her back and guide her along the tree line. "Look." I point to the loose dirt along the base of the tree trunk. "No tracks, the dirt looks like someone ran a rake over it. Something's up here, and I'm not leaving until I find out what the hell is happening."

Her breathing rate increases. "Are we looking at a homicide? Maybe we should call Sheriff Townsend."

Why do I get the feeling this sheriff is way more involved than he should be? "Let's check out the scene a little better first." I gravitate away from the crime scene and move to the right, a path leading to the deep woods pops into my field of vision. "Come on." I hold out my hand.

She takes it, sliding her fingers into mine. "Hope you've got a firearm in that bag of tricks, preferably one without silver bullets."

I turn to face her. "Don't worry. I'll take care of you."

"Exactly what I'm afraid of," she says, so low I almost don't hear her. Why the hell is she afraid of me? I mean, she saved me so I pretty much owe her.

I lead us down to the path and stop at some dried mud right before the thicker part of the woods start. A hiking boot print, about a men's size twelve, sits near the side of the mud patch. "Footprint but no animal print." I turn toward her, staring at her ashen face.

"Maybe it was from a hiker, nothing to do with the case."

I nod. "Maybe, except the next print is about thirty feet away." I point to a mud patch with a footprint in the middle near a rock. "Do the hikers around here jump like Spiderman, or do the animals wear hiking boots?"

She looks around the like the perpetrator is going to jump out saying "here I am". Only creature that can jump that far is a bloodsucking vamp or a werewolf, and werewolves eat more than their victim's blood.

"There's got to be some kind of explanation." She takes a step closer to me.

She's either warming up to me or scared shitless and I'm all she's got out here. I'm going to pretend it's the first one. "Yeah, there will be...it just might not be the one you're expecting." I start up the grassy path. Maybe I can spot the next boot print and have a clue where this vamp came from. "Come on, let's see what else we can find."

She grabs my hand and sticks by my side, sending the aroma of her fruity perfume through every pore in my body. Her touch jolts electric shocks to the depths of my soul. I'd do anything to protect this Goddess next to me, even if I end up in a vampire nest.

She takes a deep breath and stops cold. "Wait." She points forward like my uncle's English setter when it sees a pheasant.

I scan the area. Jesus Christ, how the hell did she see it? I let go of her hand and turn to face her. "Stay here." I pull my Colt 45 from the holster tucked in the back of my jeans and sweep the woods from side to side. Cora trembles, pressing her lips together so she doesn't let out the slightest peep.

I walk slowly, grabbing the blood soaked leaf Cora spotted. Okay, the vamp either left a trail for his buddies or didn't clean up as good as he thought. I walk around to the left, in the thickest part of the woods, my heart pounding with every step.

Leaves rustle like a cyclone suddenly formed a few feet from me. I take off like a bat out of hell, holding my Colt in front of me. Flashes of color sweep by the cloudy woods, leaving nothing but streaks through the sky. I stop, standing with my back against the tree, trying to control my breathing. The woods quiet down, the beating of my heart the only sound pounding through my brain.

I scan the tree line. Nothing as far as the eye can see. The eerie silence sends chills from my spine to my ankles. Déjà vu floods through me, taking me back to the day I followed Ruby down the deep row of cornfields. The bloodsucker was waiting there for her and she ran to him like a damn teenager who watched Twilight too many times. I managed to throw a syringe of dead man's blood at him like a dart but Ruby ripped it out before it had a change to destroy the leech. Whatever spell she's under, I'll find her and fix it even if it's the last thing I do. A cool breeze flows across my face bringing me back to reality. I wait a few minutes, trying to catch a glimpse of something...anything. *Goddammit*, it's gone without a trace. I lower my weapon and let my muscles relax.

Jesus, Cora's still out there. Adrenaline flows, clouding all judgement. I spring to action and rush through the woods, getting hit with branches and leaves on the way. *Please tell me the vamp didn't get her.* How the hell can I be so careless?

I should've listened to Zane at that vamp bar years ago. Taught me everything I know about the bloodsuckers. Plus one important rule: work alone and don't get attached to anyone...it will only get one of you killed. Why the hell don't I listen?

I stop at the opening to the thick brush right where I left her. I do a quick 360 trying to catch any glimpse of her fiery red hair, or that sweet smell that draws me in like a fly to honey. Nothing, it's like she disappeared into thin air.

She sure as hell is no damsel in distress. If the vamp grabbed her, she'd fight with everything she's got and definitely scream, especially since we're in the middle of a murder investigation. Nah, she's here somewhere. I can feel it.

"Cora!" I yell loud enough for her to hear but quiet enough to avoid every animal in the woods from booking it.

I wander down the path to the cleaned-up scene where the first body was discovered. Not a trace of her. Maybe she went back to the car? I mean, it's a hike but she could've gone all Incredible Hulk on me and made it in five minutes flat.

I scan the crime scene one more time looking for any slight clue that could lead me to the vamp or the nest. I circle the tree trunk like a shark about to attack. Son of a bitch...nothing. Okay, vamp is on the backburner for the moment. I need to make sure Cora is safe.

I navigate the rocky path back to the car. Pain radiates through my feet like I walked across a bed of nails. God dammit, I'm going to have to invest in a pair of Herman Survivors for this case. I make it halfway down the hill and stop dead.

Leaves crunch, sending echoes through the still woods. I grip my Colt and hold it out in front of me. Twigs snap, the sound getting closer with each passing second. I take a deep breath to even my heartrate. Arrogant bastard came back. I'll blow him into next week and follow it up with a dead man's blood cocktail...once I get the intel I need.

My legs tremble as adrenaline rushes through my brain, numbing my body. I put pressure on the trigger, waiting for my target to emerge. A dark figure slowly moves toward me, coming into focus.

"Dex, is that you?" Cora steps out of the tree line and gasps.

I let out the breath I didn't know I was holding and lower my arms. "What the hell are you thinking? I could've killed you." I tuck the Colt back in my holster.

"Sorry, I thought you could differentiate between a person

and an animal...my mistake." She folds her shaking arms across her chest. "Did you see it?"

I shake my head. "Got away before I could get a good look...you?"

"No, but check this out." I walk up to her, the sweet nectar of her essence flowing through my body. I breathe her in, taking a big hit like a drug I can't get resist.

She hops up an embankment like a gazelle. I follow her lead, watching the scarlet strands of her long hair flow in the breeze like wildfire. We walk a worn dirt path to another section of woods that thins. She stops and points at a blueberry bush.

"Look." She pulls down a bough of leaves.

Red droplets cover the greenery. Holy shit, we interrupted the vamp mid-feed. I bend down and eye the fresh blood.

"You've got an eye for blood." It's like she has this sixth sense to detect it.

"In my line of work, blood tells a lot." She scoots next to me and follows the red trail to a few blades of grass underneath the bush. "It looks like the victim...or whatever...moved here."

I stand up and scan the dirt. The bastard had no time to clean up his mess. Maybe now we can find some answers. "Come on...the trail keeps going." I spot a vague footprint in the loose dirt. A few drops of blood lie near it.

She marches up to me and looks around, breathing in the air like a blood hound. Her porcelain skin glows against the faint hints of sunlight creeping in the dark forest. I stare, captivated by her being. She stops dead, like a missile finding a target.

I focus on her face and follow her gaze. She gasps and puts her hand to her mouth. "Oh my God, Dex."

"Don't move. Call the sheriff."

3

COLLABORATION

"Dear God, I've never seen anything like this." Sheriff Townsend paces the area nibbling on an unlit cigar. "No animal short of a grizzly makes this kind of mess."

"More like a great white shark," I say.

Is he for real? There's the same probability of seeing either one in these woods. I watch the last hints of sunlight reflect off of the dark puddle of blood like shooting stars in the night sky. It's kind of beautiful in a sick, twisted way.

Sheriff Townsend dips a twig in the blood puddle, mixing it around like he's making a mud pie. "What do you think about this?" He turns toward me.

"I think you're contaminating a crime scene." The words drip from my mouth more harsh than I attended. Jesus, what academy did he graduate from? I mean, yeah it's a small town...I get it, but he's acting like he's covering up the crime. Hell, maybe it is him.

"I'll have Deputy Silveri rope the area off with caution tape." He pulls the cigar from his mouth. "Mountain lion? It's something that took the body with it. Any ideas?"

"A few. I need more evidence first." I know exactly what did this, and it's not anything with a heartbeat. "A body would help."

"I was an Eagle Scout. Let's see if my tracking skills are still up to par." The sheriff fiddles with a few leaves and takes off into the woods.

God, I hate small town cops. It's like they haven't been trained in anything more serious than writing a parking ticket. He's got two bodies, no suspects, no motives, just blaming some mystery animal. Besides that, he's digging in the only evidence available with a stick? I take a deep breath and slowly exhale. Okay, I see the men in blue are no help, so it's up to me to save the day.

I run my eyes along the edge of the puddle. A few broken twigs and a bush missing a slew of leaves that were probably ripped off grace the edge of the worn path. The vamp chased the victim up the path and bit something major right here. But not major enough to stop them. A brief struggle took place near this bush where the leaves are missing, and a few splattered blood droplets stick to the couple of leaves that remain. Looks like the vamp went all Dracula next and grabbed the victim then jumped, taking the victim somewhere else to end it all.

I search the woods that are getting darker by the second. Cora swings her head around, looking for something...anything that would close this case. This vamp is seasoned but something happened. Why would a vamp clean up one crime scene until it's near spotless and leave a puddle of blood in the next?

It's fucking with me. No other explanation. Maybe I've actually found the vamp nest I'm looking for, and can finally get Ruby out of her disaster of a situation. I pull a flashlight from the inside pocket of my leather jacket and shine it along the perimeter of the soon-to-be crime scene.

"Dex...I think I found something." Cora gestures for me to

meet her near the end of the path Sheriff Townsend took. She points to a silver bangle bracelet.

Nice. The victim found out vamps hate silver. She must've burned the bastard with it just enough to run. I'd like to think she made it out alive but based on the blood puddle and what I know about these undead assholes, she has no chance in hell.

Sheriff Townsend emerges from the trees, sporting a pathetic smile. "Cora, nice work. You know there's always a place for you on the force."

Seriously, dude? You come here, pollute the crime scene, formulate ridiculous scenarios on what may have caused these murders, and then hit on the coroner whose IQ is probably triple yours? God, he must be clinically insane. I peruse the wrinkled uniform that's way too tight in the waist, shifting my eyes to his uneven mustache that makes him look more like a 70's porn star than a sheriff.

She doesn't even flinch. "I've got my fill of work," she says without taking her eyes off of the area near the bracelet. "No tracks of any kind, just the pool of blood and the bracelet. If I didn't know better, I'd think this was a suicide. You know... expect when you succeed you can't hide the body."

Twilight sets in, sending moonlight shining down on Cora. The fiery highlights in her hair gleam, like midnight fire. I take a deep breath, taking her in. Dear God, she drives me insane. What's her deal? I get that she doesn't like Townsend—or should I call him Rosco? Am I losing my touch or does she like the whole hard-to-get deal? I'm not a quitter so I hope she's ready for the Dex Jagger charm.

"Which arteries can cause this much blood loss in a puddle?" After years of chasing vamps, I got this one down, but any reason to let Cora show me her skills can only help me get on her good side, right?

"Most likely jugular or femoral. I doubt whatever did this could access the aorta without a lot more blood splatters." She nibbles her lip.

Hmm, do I make her nervous or does she know more about this case than she's letting on? "Once we find the body, we'll see if the injuries match the others. Then we'll know if we have a serial killer on our hands."

Sheriff Townsend wrinkles his forehead and jerks his head back. "You mean a serial animal attacker." He walks down the small hill back to Cora and me. "We don't have any murders in our town."

Okay, dude. However you want to play this. "You should put that on a sign coming into town."

Sheriff Townsend walks up to me, puffing out his chest like a fat bald eagle. "If it's not an animal, what exactly are you still doing here?"

Great, a pissing contest. If he's trying to impress Cora, he's going to look really bad when I knock him on his ass in two seconds flat. I'm ready to fight a vamp who's ten times as strong as me, and can kill me more ways than I can count. Does he seriously think I'm afraid of a small town cop? Jesus, he probably never even shot that Glock in his holster.

I stand tall, staring directly into his dark beady eyes. "Can't leave without a full report and I'll need a suspect or murder weapon to rule out anything else. If you can't do your job, guess I'll have to stick around and do it for you."

A low growl forms in his throat and his nostrils flare. The sky darkens, casting shadows along his scarlet cheeks. He opens his mouth to say something but nothing comes out.

Cora moves between us. The aroma of sweet honey resonates through me, calming me like someone shot Valium into my veins. I look past her to Sheriff Townsend. Guess her perfume has the same effect on him. He lets out a deep breath and takes a step back.

"We need to work together to solve this case. So maybe cut down the testosterone." She runs her hands through her hair.

"Sorry, babe. I'm all man." I sneer at Sheriff Townsend.

He shakes his head. "Let's solve this quick so he can get back to chasing squirrels."

I charge forward, pressing against Cora. She pushes on my chest with both hands. Within seconds, I'm at ease. Jesus, is she drugging me or something?

I take a deep breath. "It's getting dark, whatever is doing this has the upper hand at night. Especially the animals."

"Thought you said it wasn't an animal." Sheriff walks past me, looking over his shoulder.

Funny. "If the town doesn't have any murderers it's got to be a monster...or an alien... You pick." If he only knew what exists he'd shit right in those navy polyester pants.

He turns his head and keeps walking like he didn't even hear me. Cora folds her arms over her chest. Yeah, I get it. I'm probably pissing her off more than anything but she'll think about my antics all night. At least she's thinking about me.

She struts forward, weaving her way through the small trees. Her hair blows in the breeze, flowing like a mermaid on land. A split second later, she trips over a tree root and pummels forward. I catch her right before her face plants itself in the cold dirt.

"Don't fall for me." I flash a smile.

She stands and brushes herself off. "Why? You taken?"

"You interested?" I slowly move my hand away.

"Not even a little." Her voice shakes. She takes off in front, watching her footing as she navigates the rocky path.

Even though I hear the regret in her tone, I think I'm starting to grow on her. "Don't knock it till you try it, babe."

She huffs and marches ahead to catch up with Sheriff Townsend. Hate to break it to her but he probably jacks off to her every night. Plus, if a vamp shows up, he'd be as helpful as grease on a fire.

"Come on, I'm kidding." I quicken my pace to keep up with them.

Clouds sweep in, sending darkness over the moonlight. The forest turns into a land of dark shadows. A breeze flows through, rustling the leaves just enough to make my adrenaline kick in. I turn from side to side, sweeping the tree line for any signs of an intruder.

"Got a flashlight, sheriff?" Maybe he's useful for something.

"Sorry, left it in the car," he mumbles.

Really? Looks like I have to do everything around here. I dig for my cell phone in my pocket and click on the flashlight app. The bright beam illuminates the path just enough. I send the light toward Cora.

My feet throb against the motorcycle boots, which are turning on me. Guess the whole, beauty is painful saying is true. Second best thing to being with Cora, lying with my feet up drinking a beer in my hotel room. And that's the plan once we make it out of here.

Sheriff Townsend slows to a stop. "Ugh, can I use your phone to call the deputy? I forgot mine in the car."

Wow, he is a piece of work. Should I wipe his ass for him too? "Here, knock yourself out."

Cora looks at me and smirks like she knows exactly what I'm thinking: how the hell is he going to help us with this investigation? I mean, he's more of a burden than anything else.

He dials the phone. "Silveri. I need you up here ASAP to rope off a crime scene. We're in the woods near the other scenes. I'll wait for you by the bridge." He fidgets with his fingers. "Yeah, and bring a flashlight."

I press my lips together, trying to prevent the hundreds of slide one-liners from falling out of my mouth. I grab my cell phone and take the lead, letting the dim light be our beacon.

Cora catches up to me, leaving Sheriff douchebag behind us. "What are we looking at here?"

I focus on her perfect face. "An angel." It slips out of my mouth before my brain realizes.

"Would it kill you to professional for a minute?" She gives me that are-you-for-real look.

"Might." I snicker. "Kidding." I angle the flashlight so the path lights up in front of Cora. "Hard to say without a body. Lots of things can cause excessive bleeding but to have that much blood in one puddle, no victim, and no trail of blood anywhere else...you got me."

"Nothing your bag of tricks can take care of?" She looks down at the ground.

I stop and turn toward her. "What does that mean?"

She shrugs. "I guess we need to look at all the possibilities." She starts walking again as the Sheriff catches up.

I need to get her alone, and not for the usual reason. If she knows what anything in my duffle bag kills, then she's either a hunter or a victim. I replay the events of the bike crash in my head. Was she really just passing or did she want to end the vamp responsible for this too?

"Maybe we can discuss our theories over coffee. You up for it?" I ask.

The sheriff whistles "Taps", louder than necessary. Hate to break it to him, but if he keeps this shit up he'll be hearing the tune from the afterlife. Ruby would give him a run for his money. Back when we were kids, she purposely did things to aggravate me: snapping her gum while I was studying, repeating everything I said—hell one time she showed up at the drive-in when I was on date with Pam Winston and sat between us. Once I was about to lose my shit, she'd flash those puppy dog eyes and schoolgirl smile and I'd instantly forgive her. Did the vamps take that away too? I'll kill those sons of bitches.

"I prefer to discuss it in my office...but I do have coffee." Cora struggles to hold back the smile trying to form.

Oh right, the case. "It's a date." I wink.

Sheriff Townsend clears his throat. "Silveri's here." He points to the lights coming toward us.

Great, maybe if the two of them put their brains together they'll have the intelligence of one below-average human. "Can you guys close this area off to the public? Hikers should stay away until this case is solved."

"We can do anything. We're the law here," Sheriff Townsend says.

And he's humble too. Just what this town needs: an idiot on a power trip. Deputy Silveri parks behind Cora's Beemer and steps out of the car. He slaps a tan hat on his head that makes him look more like a cowboy than a Rick Grimes.

He walks toward us, handing us each a flashlight, and stops at Cora. "What did you find?"

She opens her mouth to speak but Sheriff Townsend steps in front of her. "Massive amount of blood at the end of the dirt trail."

Silveri shifts his gaze toward me. "You the fish and wildlife officer?"

"In the flesh." I scan him from head to toe like the terminator making my assessment. He's young, maybe in his early twenties, with one of those baby faces that makes him look like a teenager. He seems to have more brains than his boss; maybe he can help with the case or at least not get in my way.

"What kind of animal does this?" He shines his flashlight through the dark woods.

"Saber tooth tiger." I smirk. "It's atypical behavior for any animal."

He nods. "Rabies?"

At least he's coming up with theories other than "we don't have murderers in this town."

I shake my head. "Cujo doesn't cover up a crime scene." I lean against a tree at the edge of the bridge. "If this is an animal attack, a person's covering up for it. Anyone around here have an unhealthy attachment to the woodland creatures?"

"No sir. Except for Cora." He turns toward her.

She puts her hands on her hips. "Are you suggesting I'm running around cleaning up crime scenes to protect a rabid animal?" She raises her voice, almost yelling.

He shakes his head. "No, ma'am. I know you help out down the animal rehabilitation center. That's all."

All girls like animals and any that don't have some degree of evil inside them. Unless, there's a shifter in our midst. Doesn't make sense, they don't drain bodies and they sure as hell don't work with vamps.

"Silveri, head up to the crime scene and rope it off. Maybe we can get more answers tomorrow in the daylight." Sheriff Townsend walks to the cruiser and grabs a roll of crime scene tape. He tosses it to Silveri. "I'll come with you, just in case the perp shows up."

So now it's a perp. Guess he's one of those morons that change his mind every two seconds so he's never wrong. Well, if the "perp" does show up they're both goners. Especially now, prime vamp feeding time.

I take a deep breath and lean forward, scraping my hand off the tree bark. I look down at the few drops of blood dripping down palm. Son of a bitch. Eh, just a flesh wound. I quickly wipe it off and another droplet forms. What the hell?

Cora rushes over. "What's wrong?"

Sheriff Townsend and Deputy Silveri stop in their tracks. "Find something?"

I move away from the tree and shine my phone flashlight up to the sky. A chill runs from my head to my toe and my heartrate triples. "Yeah, and it ain't pretty."

4

DISCOVERY

A limp arm hangs over the tree limb, pale gray and devoid of any sign of life. I focus on the red sparkly fingernails that gleam against the moonlight. Dammit, she didn't have a chance in hell. Probably some chick out for a fun night of partying and ends up meeting the wrong guy...and by some miracle it isn't me this time.

A droplet of blood falls. Cora sprints up the worn path. Jesus Christ she's like a blood hound who got a whiff of the scent. She scans the dried leaves and grass, moving like a gazelle through the dirt path.

Son of a bitch, she might run right into him. I follow her, jogging to keep up. Pain radiates from my heels to my toes. I muddle through and keep her in my sights. "Cora...wait." My raspy voice barely lifts above the sound of crunching leaves. "It could still be out there."

She runs through the forest like wood nymph on crack, and then suddenly comes to a complete stop. What is going on with her? One minute, she's hiding in the trees, the next she's busting out like a warrior fighting for justice.

I hold out my arm and catch hers. "What do you think you're doing?" I say through shallow breaths, almost panting.

"Trying to stay on the trail." She tries to pull her arm away.

I grip tighter. "Do you have a death wish?"

"I know what I'm doing, Dex."

"Can you share that with me?" I release my death grip and stop in the middle of the path.

She lifts her head and takes in the fresh forest scent. "It goes cold from here." She follows a drop of blood on the leaf of a bush and scans the area for clues. Nothing.

Why the hell is she acting like she can smell blood as good as a shark in open water? If I didn't know better, I'd think she was a vamp herself. Except for the fact I've seen her in sunlight and she didn't turn into a ball of fire. She's different...like no one I've ever met.

I take a deep breath and slowly exhale. Unique is not one of the qualities I look for in a woman. Last time I met a girl like no other: Jessica—she ended up being a Siren. When I was under her spell I almost did the unthinkable...killed Ruby. Of course, Ruby knew exactly what to do. She stabbed me in the leg with a brass knife and then shoved it into Jessica's heart. A split second later, the spell wore off and left me guilty until this day. Jesus, Ruby's a warrior. Can take down any monster she comes within ten feet of her. Why the hell would she run away with one?

"Cora, ambulance is here. They're taking the body to the morgue." Sheriff Townsend's voice crackles through the blowing leaves.

"Okay, on my way." Cora turns toward me. "You coming?"

I nod. "You gonna explain all this to me?"

She crinkles her forehead. "What are you talking about?"

"Oh honey, we're way past that. You know what I mean." I stare into her caramel eyes with gold hints flashing through.

"You plan on telling me about how you work with the Fish

and Wildlife Department? Forest rangers don't usually wear motorcycle boots on hikes in the woods." She folds her arms across her chest.

"Coroner's don't usually chase blood trails through the woods." I flash a sexy half-smile and raise my eyebrows.

She huffs and shakes her head. "You gonna be able to handle this?"

"Try me."

"Keep your hands off everything." Cora slides on a pair of rubber exam gloves. "Something tells me you hear that a lot."

I stare as she pulls the glove over her fingers. A shockwave of erotic tingles pulsate through my body. Every move she makes sends me into another dimension. "Not usually from girls." I slip on the safety goggles trying to divert any attention away from the zipper of my jeans. Unless she's got something really good in mind.

"I highly doubt that." She pulls out the medical examiner's report from the chart. "Bite marks on the right jugular area penetrating through." She turns the neck to the side. "Any idea what animal does this?"

I focus on the two hollowed-out bite marks. No animal in existence even comes close to piercing the vein of a human and draining the blood, leaving behind all the meat.

"Are we still playing this game?" I take a step back and lean against the wall, folding my arms across my chest. "You know this was no animal attack."

The dark gray walls of the morgue grow colder with each breath Cora takes. She drops the folder on a stainless steel table near the body, sending papers spreading across the shiny finish.

She steadies her trembling hands. "What exactly is your

theory...you think some monster is doing this?" She breathes heavy, like she's about to lose it. "Is that why you carry silver daggers and dead man's blood in your duffle bag?" Cora stares at me, her golden brown eyes seem to see to the depths of my soul.

Enough of the bullshit. Time to get down to business. "Maybe you should too...because there's a vamp killing people in Whispering Pines and your douchebag sheriff isn't doing squat about it. Amazing he survived this long."

She looks down at the ground, her arms trembling like she's in the Arctic Circle. "They teach you all this at Fish and Wildlife training?"

"Yep, just like they teach you this stuff in coroner school."

She lets out a sarcastic laugh and shakes her head. "I went to medical school."

Smart ass and sexy as sin. Dear God, this girl couldn't get any better if I created her myself. "So what's happening here? Is there a nest?"

She fidgets, unsure if she should drop the act and solve this case or continue with the façade. "I don't know."

Fire runs through my veins. Oh, hell no, they didn't get to her like they did Ruby. Is she protecting the bloodsuckers? "You some kind of Twilight groupie, doc?"

She sighs. "First of all, don't call me doc. You sound like Bugs Bunny. Second. No, I'm not a Twihard. I want these creatures the hell out of my town."

I move closer, her sweet scent flows through my pores. "Tell me what you know."

"You first." She stands tall, her scarlet hair falling in perfect waves along her shoulders.

Great, we're in a pissing contest. I'm a gentleman, although many wouldn't agree, I'll let her win. I take a deep breath, blowing gout my cheeks as I exhale. Okay, if she wants to know my deal, I'll give her the short version…but I need to know her story if we plan to survive.

"Woke up one morning and my parents were both dead on the floor, blood everywhere like you see in one of those budget slasher movies after the killer hacks up everyone with a chainsaw." Okay, maybe a little too graphic. Nothing like sharing my worst possible memory with someone who either can't stand me or is trying like hell to resist me. I close my eyes trying to suppress the memory to the pit of my soul.

"Was it a vampire?" Cora reaches out and touches my forearm but the fact that she can't look me in the eye tells me she knows it wasn't a vamp.

Tingles sweep through me, following the path of her fingers. It takes my worst experience to make her act semi-human toward me? Whatever, I'll go for it.

"Ruby, my sister, came downstairs and rubbed her eyes the same way she does on Christmas morning. She was only ten years old. When she focused, all hell broke loose. The scream, oh man, blood curdling doesn't do it justice. She screamed like she was burning in a lake of fire. I'll never forget that sound no matter how hard I try. I promised her I'd never let anything bad happen to her again…dammit." I run my hands over my face, dragging them down my chin.

"So you hunt vampires?" She looks at me the way you look at an executioner before he puts the noose around your neck.

What the hell is she so scared of? She clearly isn't a vamp. I mean, she's been in the sun, touched silver, no way she's a bloodsucker. What's her deal?

"It was a werewolf. Their hearts were devoured." I slide the safety glasses to the top of my head. "I hunt monsters and I won't rest until every horrid creature is abolished from the earth.

She knocks over a scalpel from the steel table with her trembling arm. "So you traced a vampire here and you plan on killing it. Then what?"

"Wish it was that simple. Ruby and I trained with my dad's friend, Uncle Chaz. He taught us how to defend ourselves and how to kill these creatures. He even destroyed the werewolves that killed our parents the day after it happened—said it was his family's business."

I let out a slight laugh and pace around the room. "Would you believe the cops tried to tell me a wolf got into our house, killed them, and then left?" I shake my head. "I asked them if they saw a girl with a red hood too. Sheriff douchebag would've been great on their team."

"Dex, I'm really sorry." Her eyes warm my entire body with one look.

"Yeah, thanks." Did she suddenly take a happy pill when I wasn't watching? "I was chasing a vamp when I crashed." I run a hand through my hair. "A few months back, Ruby showed up with a bloodsucker…Jesus I can barely say it out loud. I've got to find her and get her the hell away from them. God knows what they've done to her…or if she's even still Ruby."

Cora runs up to me and throws her arms around me. You've got to be kidding me. Chicks really fall hard for the sob story. I should use this story more often, once I save Ruby.

I bury my face in her hair, taking in the sweet scent. Instantly, I'm transported into a different time, one before all the shit went down—my happy place. I never expected a girl like Cora to know anything about creatures of the night or to sympathize with my situation. Wait…how exactly does she know about the existence of bloodsuckers?

I take a step back and loosen my grip. "When did you find out about them?"

She moves away. "A long time ago." She looks at the floor like an internal struggle is taking place in her brain.

I tip her chin up. "You'll have to give me more than that."

She locks eyes with me, sending a firestorm flowing through me. I adjust my stance trying to prevent my zipper from bursting open and flying across the room.

"A vampire attacked my gram when she took me out to pick berries in the forest. Gram fought him off until I had a chance to get away. When I went back, she looked lifeless. Her skin pure white with bite marks on her neck. The vampire was nowhere to be found." She fights back the tears welled up in her eyes. "When I saw what was going on here, I knew exactly who killed those poor girls. I thought I could destroy it, maybe even get a little revenge but they're much stronger than I thought." A stray tear falls down her cheek.

I wipe it away, grazing my thumb along her cheek. "You got me, and whether you want to believe it or not, we're awesome together." Okay, so we just met but it's not like many other girls bring me to my knees and know about the underworld of monsters in existence. We're a match made in heaven.

She lets out a chuckle and forces a smile. "Yeah, we've been standing in front of a dead body talking like there's all the time in the world. For all we know, the vampire could be on his next victim."

"How do you know it's a he?" I grab a sheet of the report from the silver tray.

"He's sloppy. Left this at the crime scene." She reaches in her pocket and hands me a matchbook.

I hold it up to the light and peruse the letters, *Thunder Saloon*. "So it looks like the vamp likes to knock back a few cold ones...and I won't turn you in for withholding evidence." I wink.

"Yeah, and I won't turn you in for impersonating an officer... or the many other laws I'm sure you've broken so far." She shrugs. "Guess we won't know what the connection is between the vamp and the bar unless we go there."

"Are you asking me out?" I raise my eyebrows.

She rolls her eyes. "Not unless hell froze over, or there are flying pigs floating across the sky."

"Don't knock it till you tried it, babe." I flash her that sexy smile chicks can't resist. She doesn't react. "Back to work." I leaf through a few papers in the report. "It says here the first victim's brain matter was removed."

She folds her arms across her chest like she's warming herself in the middle of a snow storm. "Maybe a zombie vamp." She flashes a meek smile.

"Cute...ya know, I kind of like you when you're not insulting me or trying to run me out of town."

"Don't get used to it." She winks.

5

BACK IN THE SADDLE

"Safest thing you'll ever have between your legs." I rev the engine of my black Harley Davidson Fatboy.

She looks me up and down. "Yep, that's probably true." She smirks and playfully hits my arm. "I'm just your chauffer anyway. Your bike is fixed; looks like you don't need me anymore."

"Not true, we're a team." Truth is, I kinda like having her around. She beats me to the ground with her sharp tongue and can lift me to the heavens with one look. The scent of her skin blasts my body into oblivion. Can't wait to see what happens next.

Maybe I miss Ruby, but I know it's more than that. I mean, I've never met anyone in the world like Cora. I'm not ready to let her walk out of my life, plus I need help with this case...whether or not I want to admit it.

"I'm pretty sure Van Helsing works alone." She waves and turns, walking away. Her hair flows like leaves blowing in the wind, spreading the smell of her fruity perfume through the air.

"You know Van Helsing was a doctor. So I need one."

She stops and looks back over a shoulder. "I can take you to the hospital. Lots of them there." She raises her eyebrows.

"Funny. Come on, one ride. I promise you'll love it." I pull the bike a few feet closer to her.

"That's what I'm afraid of." She presses her lips together like she didn't want those words to spill from her lips.

"Take a ride on the wild side." I flash that sexy smile that's made more than a few panties drop. "If you think you can handle it." Aha, a challenge. She'll never resist it.

She folds her arms over her chest. "Do you think I can't handle you?"

I shrug. "Can't wait to find out." I wink and slide on my sunglasses.

She jumps on the back of my bike like I just double-dog-dared her to burn some rubber with me. "Let's see how fast this baby can go."

Oh, she's all in. I fire the throttle and take off, skidding and leaving a trail of rubber. Cora slides her arms around me, pulling tight like she's holding on for dear life. Believe me, she's not the only one scared of whatever the hell's going on between us. One fact, this was the best idea of my life so far.

Her hair flies in an array of directions, whipping across my face like Wonder Woman's lasso. Is it bad that I like it? She can crack me with whatever she conjures up in that brilliant mind of hers. I slow the bike to somewhere near the speed limit and Cora releases her grip. No reason to rush this. Who the hell knows how long it will last?

"Whad'ya think? Exhilarating, right?" I yell over the roar of the engine.

"A little kick-ass music and it would be perfect," she yells in my ear.

I sing the first few lines of "Strutter". "I know...a thing or two about her."

"On second thought, maybe we should stick to the sounds of the road."

I tip my head back slightly. "Are you saying you don't like my angelic voice?"

"Let's just say I doubt you'll be winning any karaoke contests. Maybe you should stick to the vampire hunting."

"I was hoping to become your personal driver." If I can find any reason to be closer to Cora, I'm there.

"Yeah, except I know your track record. Although I'll give you a pass since you were chasing a vampire." She lets out a slight gasp like she can't believe the filter from her brain to her mouth disappeared.

"Wait...what?" I slow to a snail's pace and stop at the stop sign. "How did you know that? Did you see it?"

"I...yeah. I saw it run off when you crashed. Dark brown, shoulder length hair, fangs—you know...the usual."

"And you decided not to tell me this until now?"

She shrugs. "I didn't know how you'd react."

I grip the throttle so hard the bike spatters forward. Seriously? I could've been on his tail. She pretty much witnessed the whole thing. "Where did he go? You know, after the crash?" Jesus, she could've tailed him, found out where the nest is and ended this whole deal.

"I tracked him to the edge of town." She pulls her hair back and twists it into a bun. "Dex, I couldn't leave you there to die. I had to let him go. It was catch him or save you."

I hold back a smile. "I get it...you couldn't resist my hot body."

She smacks my arm. "Are you always this much of an ass?"

I shake my head. "Nope, I'm usually much worse." A car approaches behind us. Of course once I start getting somewhere with her divine intervention has to ruin it on me. "Let's check out our lead."

I fire up the engine and take off down the road. Trees line the perimeter of the long stretch of highway, boasting their thick green leaves. I take a deep breath trying to rejuvenate myself, but the essence of Cora spreads through me like a virus. If I live to be a thousand years old I'd never forget that scent.

Shit, neither would a vamp. Is the bloodsucker here for Cora, setting traps along the way? Jesus Christ, she probably didn't even think that might be a possibility. Probably because she has no clue she can bring the devil to his knees with one look.

She wraps her arms around me, holding her body close to mine. My heart rate triples, skipping beats and creating an erratic rhythm. If she keeps this up, she'll be seeing me in the morgue after I succumb to cardiac arrest. I take a deep breath, trying to bring my body back to normal. Yeah, like that'll happen.

I turn a corner and pull into a gravel parking lot on the right. I shut down the engine and sit still in the seat. If she wants to hold me like this I'll sit here forever.

She slowly slides her hands, grazing my abs as she moves away. I wiggle in my seat trying to camouflage the bulge in my jeans.

She gazes at the wooden building that looks more like a hunting cabin than a biker bar. "Must be a hell of a business."

"Yeah, and bikers love gravel." I pull out the kickstand with my foot and walk around the parking lot. Not another car or bike in sight. Small windows grace the front of the building, covered in a thin layer of dust. Okay, so no nest here. They'd never survive the light.

Cora walks by my side and we make our way up the two steps to the black iron door. *Knock knock.* I pound my fist against the door.

No answer. I glare at my watch—two in the afternoon. Guess they do their business as night. I rub dust off of the window with my thumb and peek inside. An array of tables spread across the floor with a stage to the left and a huge bar the size of the back wall across from the entrance. Nothing fancy but still nice.

"Must be the best bar in town." I search for signs of vampire activity.

"Maybe the tri-county area." We are literally in the middle of the woods. Really creeps me out." She takes a step back.

"Ah, does this place give you the heebie-jeebies?" I say in my best Freddy Kruger voice.

"Probably just you giving them to me."

"There's the Cora I'm used to." I take a step back and pace the length of the porch. "Makes sense, vamps like to hide in the darkest areas, black as their disgusting souls."

"Guess we need to come here at night." She runs her fingers through her tangled hair.

"Are you asking me out?" I hold back a smile.

"As far as I'm aware, hell hasn't frozen over so, no."

I love it that I can get her panties in a bunch without even trying.

Cora jumps, pulling her cell phone out of her pocket.

"If we did go out on a date, you wouldn't need to keep that on vibrate anymore." I wink.

She rolls her eyes and presses accept. "Sheriff Townsend."

Ugh, not this douche again. He probably fell and stepped in the crime scene again. Or maybe he ran over a squirrel and needs to identify the official cause of death.

"Okay, we'll be right there...yeah, me and Dex." She stays silent for a minute. "We're working on the case together. You know, testing out the theories of what animal is responsible."

I can just imagine the bullshit he's feeding into her mind about me. That son of a bitch better not try to turn her against me. He has no idea what he's dealing with, not with the case, and sure as hell not with me. I'll knock him into next week if he runs his mouth. "Is there a problem?" I say in a louder voice than anticipated.

She shakes her head. "Yeah, I know the place. Off of Butler Road. Why?" She looks at the ground, trying to avoid possible eye contact with me.

What's her problem? One second we're working together and then Townsend calls, and all of a sudden she can't even speak. What's she hiding?

"See you soon," she says into the phone and shuts it off.

"Well?" I almost yell. Dammit, acting like I'm in some sort of demented competition with him sure as hell isn't going to help my chances with Cora. The son of a bitch gets under my skin, picking at my last nerve. I can barely stop myself from pummeling him, more to try to knock some sense in his backwoods arrogant brain. I've got to get a grip.

She nibbles her lip. "How fast can that hog go?"

Sheriff douchebag phones and now we have to run to his beck and call. What the hell is going on here? I mount the bike and gesture for Cora to jump on behind me. "Hold on tight, babe. Let's see."

THE ENGINE RIPS through the silent forest, sending a myriad of birds soaring through the sky, trying to escape. I slow the bike to a stop, turning my wheels just enough to fling a few small rocks at sheriff douchebag. He jumps back like we're in the old west and Wild Bill is shooting at his feet, making him dance. Wild Bill and I share the same warped sense of humor.

"Excuse me. You're tampering with evidence of a crime scene." He shakes some loose gravel from his shoe.

I slide out the kick stand with my boot and hop off the bike, holding out my hand to help Cora. "Sorry chief, my bad."

He shoots daggers, his stare more intense than a lion hunting down a zebra. Of course if we were in the jungle he'd be the one hanging from the tree. "What were you two doing?"

Cora scrunches her eyebrows giving him that none-of-your-Goddamn-business look. "Working the case...same as you."

I snicker, flashing a sly smile. "What's going on here?"

"Great question," he says under his breath. "Deputy Silveri came up to check the scene and search for any missed evidence."

Cora slips underneath the crime tape. My eyes gravitate toward her perfect ass outlined by those dark skinny jeans that should say "Fuck Me" on the pockets. Sheriff Townsend clears his throat so loud you'd swear he had bronchitis. Dammit, caught yet again. Doesn't matter. Cora's getting used to me. Hell, I think she might even like it.

Cora looks back over a shoulder shifting her gaze between us. She focuses on Sheriff Townsend's beady eyes. "Find anything interesting?"

"Oh, yeah. Case took a whole different direction." Sheriff keeps his eyes locked on mine like we're in the middle of a grade school staring contest. What the hell, I'm in. I squint, focusing on his dark pupils.

"Are we talking in riddles all night or do we plan on actually getting something done and solving this case?" She huffs, waving her arms at both of us. "Can you two step out of kindergarten and do your jobs? I don't get paid to babysit."

I hold up my hands. "What's the intel? I'm ready to catch this jerk." Always take the high road when it comes to chicks, unless there's no other choice. I've seen it happen a million times. They're all about the mature sensible man until the shit hits the fan, then they want the warrior who can kick ass and get shit done. I'm just waiting for my cue, but until then I'll play Cora's game.

She holds up her hands, gesturing toward the Sheriff. "Well…"

He turns his attention to her and flashes a soft smile. "Deputy saw someone hanging around the crime scene. At first, he thought it was an animal so he cocked his pistol and got ready to fire." Sheriff takes off his hat and runs his hand through his hair, placing the hat back on. "He said he saw a man peering out from behind a tree so he lowered his weapon…and then things got fuzzy."

"What do you mean? Did he have trouble identifying the suspect?" Cora slides her hands in her pockets and walks toward us.

Sheriff shakes his head. "He said he saw a flash of color, like everything was moving at warp speed and then the next minute he was on the ground."

"It took you this long to tell us!" I clench my jaw, letting out a low growl. Oh shit, the vamp got him. Goddammit the kid had no idea what was coming for him. And this asshole let him go back to a murder scene alone? Son of a bitch, I should've been there. I charge toward Sheriff Townsend, grabbing his shirt near the collar. "Were there any bite marks?"

Sheriff pushes against my chest but I barely move. "He hit his head off a tree. Before he went unconscious he radioed for help. I didn't inspect him for injuries. Not my job."

"Maybe if you were doing your job instead of putting all your work on the kid he wouldn't be laying in a hospital bed, you lazy bastard." Adrenaline flushes through my veins. My arms shake like they're going to explode. Dear God, stop me from adding another body to the crime scene. Even though he deserves it.

Cora rushes over and pulls us apart like she's a secret jujitsu master in her spare time. "Enough. Did he see who the person was? Give a description?"

Sheriff takes a deep breath, probably to calm his hatred and forget all the different ways he'd like to kill me. "All he said was white male, around twenty-four years old, dark shoulder length hair and…"

"And…" Cora's intense stare burns through the dark night.

"You sure you're a coroner, not a detective?" He lowers his gaze.

She relaxes her tense muscles. "Sometimes physical features can be indicative of certain diseases. I want to find out what we're dealing with here."

He nods. "He said his eyes were red."

I cover my face with my hands, slowly dragging them down my chin. Jesus Christ, he was close enough to see his eyes and still managed to live. I pace around the dirt path in front of us like a lion in a cage.

"Guess your services aren't needed anymore since no animal evidence was found." Sheriff Townsend stands tall and puffs out his chest like a demented rooster.

I stop dead and clench my fists into tight balls. Two seconds, that's all I need to pummel this son of a bitch to oblivion. The bastard sends the kid to do his dirty work and almost gets him killed. Instead of worrying about Silveri and catching this vamp, he wants to get rid of me so he can fuck Cora. This guy's worse than the vamp and Cora wouldn't fuck him if he was the last man on earth. She's way too smart for his bullshit.

Cora jumps forward, stepping between us. "Whoever's doing this could have been bitten, or come in contact with an animal that has a disease, like rabies or a mutation of the Ebola virus that might make their eyes bleed. I need him."

The words melt my soul. Maybe because for the first time in my life I feel the same way, and for reasons I can't begin to understand.

"Whatever, I'm headed to the hospital to see if Silveri remembers any more." He points directly at me just out of arm's length. "You lay a hand on me again I'll have you arrested for assaulting an officer." He walks away.

"If that's what you want to call yourself." The words slip out of my mouth before I have a chance to catch them.

He stops, standing still for a few minutes and then walks away. I get it, he wants the girl more than he wants to solve the case, and in his eyes I'm the one thing standing in his way. Hate to break it to him, but Cora has more sense than to hook up with Barney Fife. I have to give him some credit. At least he has the sense to prevent his mouth from writing a check his ass can't cash.

Cora rushes over as soon as he pulls away in the cruiser. She grabs my arm, jerking me toward her. "What the hell was that?"

Her fierce grip on my biceps sends blood rushing though my veins so loud a vamp within ten miles could hear. I flex my muscle, giving her a taste of what she could have, once she realizes she wants it.

I let out a deep breath. "I should've been here."

She releases her grip, dropping her arms. "No way we could've known."

"That kid had no idea what was out there. If I only knew Sheriff Asshole was sending him back alone, I could've..." I run both my hands through my hair.

She grabs my cheeks and turns my face toward her. "What?"

Our eyes lock. I stare at the gold flecks shining brighter than the sun. "Took the vamp down and prevented him from getting bit. Done...something. The kid walked into a twelve-gun execution with no clue what exists in the dark shadows, and I failed him."

She pushes her forehead against mine. "Not true, and you don't know he's been bitten. He hit his head hard; it could be a concussion." She slides her hand along my cheek. "He's not Ruby."

I close my eyes and breathe in the sweet fruity scent that swarms around Cora like a cloud burst. Her breathing increases. I hold onto her waist, pulling her closer. "I need to save them both." My lips graze hers when I speak.

"You can't save the world, Dex." Her heart beats like a jackhammer, vibrating through her chest.

"I can save you." I press my lips against hers.

She slides her hands around the back of my neck. *I was Made for Loving You* blares through the air. Cora jumps back like she's just tasted the venom of a rattlesnake. She pulls her cell phone out of her pocket and stares at the screen until it goes to voicemail. "I gotta go." She takes three steps back.

You've got to be kidding me, although I admire the random KISS song choice that fate picked as Cora's ringtone. Maybe the Gods are on my side. Note to self, though: never set my ringtone to shuffle. Doubt it would work out this well twice.

"You sure you wanna go?" I take a step toward her.

She wraps her arms around her chest liked she's holding herself together. Her body trembles. What the hell is she so afraid of? She nods. "I have to."

Okay, no sense in pushing her away any further. It's probably Sheriff douchebag. Does he have some kind of freaky radar? "Hang on, I'll take you home."

She looks around like there's some other option. It's hop on the hog or walk. Either way I'm not letting her leave alone.

She crawls on the back of the bike like she's on her way to the electric chair. "Dex..." Her voice is a whisper.

For the first time in my life I shut my mouth, staying silent. Nothing but the roar of the engine filling the air. Whatever's going on in her head won't break this. Not as long as I have a few more tricks up my sleeve.

6

MIDDLE OF NOWHERE

"Think of it as going undercover." I lean against the doorjamb trying to peel my eyes away from the cleavage peeking out from her deep V-neck black shirt. Goddammit, the brain of Stephen Hawkings, and a body that could make any playboy centerfold run to the nearest surgeon for a touch-up.

"I didn't study sting operations in medical school." She steps out from behind her desk.

I focus on her dark blue skinny jeans, traveling down her legs that seem to go on for miles, to her stiletto boots with studs lining the back. Holy fuck, if I don't get in a brawl tonight I'll call it a miracle. Every guy in there with a dick can't ignore her.

"Summon your inner Julia Roberts." I should be the one winning the academy award since I totally acted like last night didn't even happen. Doesn't matter, I wouldn't know what to say anyways. Chicks read into things like there's a secret treasure map etched in my words.

"Are you saying I look like a prostitute...you know, like in Pretty Woman?" She looks down at her outfit and takes a step back. "That's it, I'm changing."

I grab her arm before she walks out of reach. "You look perfect." I soften my grip. Truth be told, she could wear a burlap sack and be the most beautiful woman in the room. She's got to know that. I mean, she's not blind.

"Come on. Let's go before I change my mind." She marches through the hall of her office to the door.

My eyes glue to her ass like the Terminator when he zeros in on a target. Jesus Christ, throw her on a billboard from this angle and the stock in those jeans would skyrocket. No way in hell I'm making it through tonight unscathed.

She looks over a shoulder. "You coming?"

I suppress the urge to say *not yet* and jerk my head back, pulling myself into reality. "Lead the way." I gesture toward the door and follow her, closing the door behind me. We step onto the sidewalk and stop dead.

She points toward the motorcycle. "No way I'm getting on that thing at night. I've seen you drive it in the dark before. Not a good memory."

"Come on, doc. You know we need to play the part. Can't go to a biker bar with no bike. Dead giveaway." I fire up the engine and rev the throttle.

She huffs, probably more because she knows I'm right. "Don't call me that."

"No problem, red." I bite my lip holding in a smirk.

"Can't you call me Cora?"

"Not tonight, babe." She loves it when I get on her nerves, whether she wants to admit it or not.

"God, you're impossible." She hops on the back on the bike and wraps her arms around me.

"Oh, I'm just getting started." I pull away from her office like a bat out of hell.

∼

"Don't be offended if I call you my old lady." I kill the engine and slide off the bike.

"Every word that comes out of your mouth offends me. I'm used to it." She flings her leg over the bike like she's patented the move.

I let out a loud moan and adjust my jeans to hide the bulge forming. Harleys line the mammoth parking lot. I mean, there's got to be at least a hundred of them. Last time I saw this many bikes was when I found a nest near Sturgis. I put my hand in the small of her back and guide her forward.

She squirms away. "Don't see any other bikers treating their old ladies," she makes quotation marks in the air with her hands, "like they're about to board a yacht."

I pull my hand away and smack her ass. "Better?"

She rolls her eyes and continues forward. I stick close to her side. The fruity scent stings my senses, turning me into a horny teenager. Her hair swings over her shoulder as she walks sending my nerve ending into a frenzy. Gold flashes of glitter follow each strand of hair. Jesus Christ, her hotness is making me hallucinate. I rub my eyes and walk alongside of her.

"Your perfume is sending me into anaphylaxis."

"I don't wear perfume," she says quietly, and slips her hands into her jean pockets.

Dammit, I offended her for real this time. "Then you're great vamp bait." Son of a bitch. What the hell is wrong with me? I'm awesome with the lines. Maybe her essence renders my brain inactive.

"Don't kill me with the compliments." She flashes me a side eye and pulls open the door.

Smoke bellows out like the place is on fire. I cough a few times until my lungs adjust. Cora shoots me a dirty look as if I've just blown our cover. Maybe the foul stench will cover up her shampoo, or whatever that sweet smell is that sticks to her body.

Dozens of men dressed in jeans and leather vests line the bar; a few shoot pool from the billiard tables near the back wall, and the rest gather toward the stage. Maybe there's some stripper show coming up. Cora will love that one. Pretty much everyone except me is wearing a cut—from the Outlawed Devils, Satan's Soldiers, to Reapers Revenge. Jesus Christ, I'm like one of the wild hogs.

"Here's an open one." Cora grabs my wrist and guides me toward a table near the wall. Out of the way but close enough to see everything.

I follow her like a moth to a flame. "Okay, here's the plan." I plop into the chair. "See who you find that fits the deputy's description."

She hops into the chair and glares around the bar, waving her hand in front of her face to clear the smoke hovering in the air. "That's pretty much everyone."

"Uh, yeah. Most of these guys are older, at least in their thirties. The guy we're looking for is young." I shift my gaze along the dark gray walls trying to stay inconspicuous. "Think. Is the spot where the bodies were found significant in any way? Does it mean anything?"

A waitress, maybe in her late twenties wearing a leather mini skirt and painted on white T-shirt, makes her way to our table. "What'll ya have?"

"Beer for me." I lean back in my chair taking another look around.

"Grey Goose martini, extra dirty." Cora's eyes widen. She just realized what she said. "How about Jack and Coke?"

"Coming right up." The waitress squints her forehead and scurries back to the bar.

"Really?" I swear she's trying to get me killed.

"Sorry, momentary lapse." She shifts her eyes from the stage to the bar and then back to me. She gasps like a lightbulb just went off in her head. "Years ago, before the bridge went out, the spot where the victims were found was the place to go parking. But that was a long time ago."

I raise an eyebrow. "Any personal experience you care to share?"

"Not with you."

The waitress brings our drinks and sets them on the table. "Anything else for you, sugar?"

I hold up my hands. "I'm good." A small smile bursts from my lips.

"I bet." She winks and walks away.

"Looks like you're getting along just fine with the locals." Cora sips her drink.

"Jealous?" I smirk.

"Yeah, I'm about to fling myself off a cliff." She rolls her eyes. "What are you thinking?"

"Sure you want to know?" If she's so repulsed by words coming out of my mouth she'll never handle the thoughts my brain conjures.

"About the case. You think the old parking spot has some kind of significance? Since when do vamps go parking?"

I lean in closer. "Maybe we should give it a whirl. Just to be sure."

She folds her arms over her chest, pushing her cleavage up so high at least twenty guys stare. Damn, I don't know how much longer I can control myself around her. "I think we might have a teen vamp."

She shakes her head. "No way, bridge has been closed for years."

"An old teen vamp." I slug my beer.

"How would he get into this bar if he was underage?"

"Newsflash, lots of kids get into bars underage. I can give you a few tips sometime."

She leans back in her chair, trying to get as far away from me as humanly possible. "I bet."

"Maybe he used to go parking there back in the day and thinks of it as the place for conquests." I give her the hell-yeah nod.

She completely ignores me and glances around the bar. "A handful of guys have shoulder-length dark hair but they're all too old to fit the description unless Silveri was wrong, or the vamp did something to make himself look older." She leans forward, glancing around the room but flashing her breasts at me. "As far as I can see everyone has a reflection in the mirror behind the bar. No red eyes either."

I try to pry my gaze away from her breasts before she notices. "A few more drinks and you may see two sets of them." I raise my head but she catches me, mid-gaze.

"As long as there's not more than one of you." She sips her drink.

"Your pure hatred for me makes me try even harder. Hope you know that."

"How about we cut the bullshit," she says between gritted teeth.

"Amen." I hold up my drink.

"And get back to work." She finishes her drink in one gulp and turns her chair so it faces the door. "He's got to be coming soon. I'll be ready when he does."

"Okay, Chuck Norris. What's the plan when you find him?"

She nibbles her lip, searching for one of those snide comments she loves to throw at me. "You do your job…stab him with dead man's blood."

I laugh. "Oh, yeah. He's probably friends with half these

guys, who have no clue what he really is, and I wouldn't get within ten feet of him."

She taps her fingers on the glass. "Fine. What's your plan?"

I finish the last of my beer, wiping the suds off my top lip with the back of my hand. "We blend in. You work your magic and get his attention."

"And how do I do that?"

I look her up and down. "Trust me, you're doing it...if you can get him out the door, I'll slip through the back and take care of him. Like a ninja."

A chuckle bursts from her lips. "Sorry...go on."

I hold up my hands. "That's it, what do you think?"

"You better be able to back up your mouth or you're going to get me killed." She waves for the waitress to bring another round.

"Don't worry about me, just hook him in. Let your body talk, not your mouth so much."

She kicks me under the table as the waitress sets down our drinks. I flinch, bending over forward. The waitress must've taken that as some sick love ritual because she flashes a smile and winks. Jesus Christ, what the hell are the girls in this town thinking?

"First, we need to blend in." I point at the Karaoke sign near the stage.

She shakes her head and holds up her hands. "Hell, no."

"Come on, no one knows us here, plus it'll be fun. I'll do it too."

She slugs her drink, finishing half the glass in one gulp. "You make an ass out of yourself all the time. Nothing new for you, and I don't want to follow suit."

"Aww there's that small town charm they talk about." I sip my beer. "You know they have KISS, right?"

"I need about ten more of these before I get up there." She raises her glass.

"We don't have that kind of time…and I have a better idea." I wave my hand toward the waitress. "Two shot glasses and a bottle of tequila."

She whips her head around when she hears my voice and gives a thumbs-up.

Cora looks at me like she's just seen a ghost. "Dear God, I've turned to the dark side."

"Don't knock it till you tried it, babe." I head over to the karaoke coordinator near the stage, keeping an eye on Cora.

"We've got spots open in a half hour." A leggy blonde hands me the master song list.

"Sign us up for two slots."

She holds up a clipboard. "Damn, can't use our real names. Come on, Dex, think. "Hunter and Bambi." Jesus Christ, those are faker than a three-dollar bill. My mind goes blank, can barely form a coherent thought.

"Gotcha." She jots down our names on the clipboard. "Call you when it's time."

I nod and head back to the table with the book. Cora stares at me, not letting her eyes leave me for a split second. Does she think I'm going to bail on her? No way in hell I'd ever leave her. No one in their right mind would.

She takes the book and flips through the pages. "Who goes first?"

"Hunter and then Bambi."

The waitress sets down the bottle of tequila and shot glasses on the table, and then quickly scurries away. Maybe Cora's death stare shook her a bit.

The heat from Cora's eyes burn through my body. "Really? Are you confusing bikers with strippers?"

I shrug. "Sorry, brain wouldn't function."

She sucks in a deep breath and loudly exhales. "Yeah, nothing new there." She stops at page ten. "Bambi will do this one... Ugh, it sounds worse when it comes out of my mouth."

"Nah, things always sound better coming from you." I leaf through the pages. "Got it."

"Care to share?" She fills her shot glass with tequila and downs the shot like it's water.

"Nope, I like to surprise you." I follow her lead and slam a shot. The liquid burns my tongue on its way down. Damn, nothing like bottom shelf liquor. I'm going to pay for this night tomorrow.

"Fine. Same here." She downs another shot.

I pull the bottle away from her. "Slow down, cowboy. You won't make it on stage if you keep that up."

"Are you saying I can't handle my liquor because I'm a girl?"

Where the hell did that come from? "No, but even a seasoned alcoholic can't drink a bottle of tequila in ten minutes without rendering themselves unconscious."

She pushes the shot glass away. "I sure as hell can't get up there sober."

"Moderation is the key." I shove both shot glasses to the side of the table and lean forward. "Trust me, once you get up there, these guys will cheer even if you sound like a cat getting a bath. You've got the hotness factor."

"Ugh, you're making me want to drink more." She bounces her knee. "Guess you have that effect on women."

"Funny. You missed your calling as a comedian."

"You give the best material." She raises an eyebrow.

"Next up, Bambi. Get down here, girl," the karaoke announcer shouts into the microphone.

Cora nibbles her lip like she's about to chew through it. She grabs the bottle of tequila and sucks it down like Ruby slugged milk out of the carton when she raided the fridge in the middle of the night.

"Let's do this." She marches to the stage.

Catcalls and whistles fill the room as she walks. I fight the urge to throat punch every guy ogling her. Doesn't matter, I'm outnumbered anyway, and she's not mine to protect.

"I Love it Loud", blasts through the PA system. Cora brings the mic to her mouth, her hand trembling right before the lyrics start. She belts out the tune as if she wrote it.

I watch her like a hawk, shifting my eyes from her red locks to the space around her body. I form my own protective shield around every inch of her, ready to pounce on anyone who invades the space. The words blur and fade away into the night. I focus on Cora, her hair sweeping from side to side as she dances to the melody of the guitar. Every move she makes draws me in a magnetic force I can't resist. Is it just me, or does everyone fall into her web?

Before I know it, she's walking off of the stage toward me. Cheers fill the air, along with high-pitched whistles and a few sexual comments I pretend I don't hear.

She hops into the seat; a smile graces her face like she just killed it at the Grammy's. "I figured a song from Creatures of the Night was appropriate. So..."

"You were freaking awesome. You sure you're a karaoke virgin?" She sucked me in and held me there hanging on her every word. No one short of Led Zeppelin can do that to me, until now.

"Not a virgin but not all that experienced." She grabs the bottle of tequila and pours a shot, sending tequila flowing over the rim onto the table. "Do a celebratory shot with me." She pulls the other shot glass toward her spilling more on the table than she gets into the glass.

Jesus Christ, she's wasted. Great, looks like we're done with our sting operation. Guess we picked the day the vamp doesn't drink. Typical.

The karaoke announcer calls for Hunter. I walk toward the stage, slow as a turtle. A few people clap but the fanfare is clearly sexist. I'll have to win them over with my charm.

"Let's rock." I grab the microphone and look out onto the crowd. "Once Bitten Twice Shy" starts to play. I morph into an eighties rocker when the guitar riff starts. Any vamp would appreciate this tune.

Cora laughs, clapping and cheering like a drunken groupie. Okay, so at this point that's pretty much an accurate assessment. I command the stage, riding the microphone stand like a horse and belting out my best falsetto. The crowd acts like I'm the best thing they've seen in years. I finish up with some air guitar and walk off the stage. Cora runs up to me and throws her arms around me. Is this still part of the act?

"Why were you holding out on me?" she slurs.

I guide her back to our table and help her into the chair. "Huh?"

"Didn't realize you were a closet rock God." She slugs tequila from a shot glass.

Well, at least she's finished downing shots. "I can rock and roll all night."

She laughs, leaning across the table toward me. "Waitress. Two beers."

"Didn't they teach you not to mix alcohols in medical school?" I turn away from her and try to catch the waitress's attention but she's already walking toward us with the beers.

Cora shakes her head. "Nope, alcohol is oxygen and a hydrogen atom. I can handle it." She takes a gulp of beer the second the waitress sets it down on the table.

"Uh-huh." I slug my beer and gesture for the waitress to

bring over the tab. The sooner I get Cora out of here the better. She'd never handle a vamp in this condition, and blowing our cover might get us both killed.

The waitress has her eyes locked on a man who just walked in the bar. He's young, with brown shoulder-length hair. Son of a bitch, it's got to be him. The waitress ignores my gestures like I turned from Brad Pitt to scum on the bottom of her shoe.

"Ma'am, we'd like our bill please." I cup my hands to for a homemade megaphone and shout across the room.

She waves her hand in the air but doesn't bother to turn around to face me. The bloodsucker has her in his grip; no way I can pull her away. I mean, even if he wasn't an undead creature, I might not pry her off a guy giving her a little attention.

The guy shifts his focus to our table. Jesus Christ, can I make possibly bring any more attention to us? Way to keep in undercover, Dex. The vamp stares at Cora as if he's dying of thirst and came across a crystal clear lake. I stand up and move around the table toward Cora.

"What do you think you're doing?" She looks up at me with glazed eyes.

Okay, so she's not as drunk as I thought. "Saving your ass. That guy over at three o'clock."

She peeks her head out from behind me. "Holy shit...it's him, right?"

"Fits the description." I sling my arm around her shoulder. "He's looking at you like Ruby when she sees a Klondike bar. He needs to know you're mine."

"When exactly did that happen?" She sits still in the chair.

"A second after he walked in here." I lean down and tuck a lock of stray hair behind her ear. The sweet scent overtakes my body, sending my heart into a plethora of erratic beats. My lips graze her earlobe as I speak. "We need to get out of here without setting him off."

"Are you insane? We finally have a chance to catch him and you want to bail?" She talks slow and quiet.

"Listen, warrior princess. You're in no shape to catch a vamp. No more tequila for you." I back up and laugh, like she just told me the funniest joke that exists. "We know who he is and where he hangs out. We'll come back and finish the job."

"Dex, I can do this." She hops off the seat to the floor, wobbling with every step.

I wrap my arm around her waist and hold her close. "Yeah, you're ready to start throwing stakes, Buffy." She tries to pull away but I hold her tight, against me. "For once in your life, will you listen to me? Not tonight."

The vamp paces around the bar, moving a few feet closer to us. I get it, he's trying to use his supersonic hearing to see what we're up to. "Shh," I whisper.

"Let's just try..."

"Shut up." Dammit, I'm not talking to Ruby. Women tend to want to punch me in the face when I demand they do anything, even if it's for their own good.

"We can still do this. I've got an idea..."

I move closer and face her. "Stop, please."

"If we head out to the dance floor, you can grab some dea..."

I slam my lips to hers stopping her midsentence. She puts her hands against my chest like she wants to fling me into the wall, but then relaxes her muscles. I slide my hands to her waist pulling her so close not even the cloud of smoke lingering in the air can fit between us. Is she into this, or is it all an act? My heart beat drums like it's about to burst out of my chest and fly across the room. She slithers her hands up my chest and interlocks them at the base of my neck, weaving her fingers in my hair. Either she really wants me or she should be standing on the stage thanking the academy.

I slide my tongue along hers, letting my hands wander to her ass. She presses herself against me harder. I grow within seconds, showing her exactly how much I want her. She moves her tongue in an array of twists and turns. I let out a low moan, breathing in her essence. Skyrockets shoot through me.

A karaoke singer screeches out a note that only dogs should hear. It pulls me back into reality. I need to stop this now or turn around and fuck her on the table.

I take a step back, pulling away. "Ready?"

She nods, more like she's giving me the okay to keep it going. If this tequila can turn women into sexy sirens I should buy a case. I toss two twenties on the table and grab Cora's hand, pulling her out the door. The vamp turns his head around like a caffeinated owl as we walking by, breathing in deep. Son of a bitch, he'll probably remember that smell for eternity.

She stumbles through the crowded space getting elbowed and pushed on the way. She scans the parking lot. "Are we close?"

Oh yeah, much closer than I ever thought possible. "You alright to hold onto me?"

She runs her tongue along her top lip. "I can do a lot more than that."

I close my eyes and exhale, trying to lower my testosterone level. My zipper presses against me like the Jaws of Life. "Tell me that when you're sober." I wanted her from the second my eyes met hers, and now I have the chance and I'm pussying out just because she had a little to drink. What the fuck happened to me?

"I'm not drunk." She kicks a leg over the seat and mounts the bike.

I scan her body from head to toe. Her painted-on jeans show off every curve of her sexy-as-hell body and that shirt lets out just enough cleavage to bring me to the brink of insanity. I press my lips together, holding in the words God- yes-let's-shack-up-right-here from my mouth and hop on the bike.

She wraps her arms around me letting her fingers graze the Promised Land. Oh, she's sure as hell not wasted. Cora knows exactly what she's doing. Do I keep it slow and steady, or take her for the ride of her life?

7

NIGHT MOVES

"I can't leave you alone tonight." I shut down the bike in the parking lot of the Overbrook Hotel.

"Good." She nuzzles up to me, pressing her face against my back.

"Come on, Cora. No one likes a tease." I squirm out of her embrace and step onto the asphalt.

"Very true. Who's teasing?" She catches her bottom lip in her teeth.

Electric shots flow through my body with the energy of a lightning bolt. Goddammit, she's wearing me down. Not that it takes much but I'm only human. How the hell did I resist her this long?

"Do I have to get you a separate room?" Okay, so most girls regret their tainted judgment the day after we hook up but I don't want Cora to be one of them. Jesus Christ, what am I saying? It's like she's neutered me. I better check those hospital records.

She puts her hand on a hip. "Sure. Just tell April, the front desk clerk, that even though I live and work in town I need a room because a vamp may be coming after me and you're the only one who can save me."

She's either the most coherent drunk in the world or she's playing it up. But why? "I'll tell her I didn't want to leave you alone because you're sloppy drunk and I need to make sure you don't choke on your own puke."

"In a different room? Do you have X-ray vision or something?" She takes a few steps closer. "Maybe you should tell her you're afraid you can't handle spending the night together."

I let out a burst of laughter. "Listen, babe. No one would believe that."

"Tell her you're all talk, no action." She leans in so close her hair caresses my cheek. "Or prove otherwise," she whispers.

Her soft breath sends chills through my body. My heart thumps against my chest. I breathe deep, trying to calm my horny-as-hell body. The sweet fruity aroma that surrounds her intensifies, sending shockwaves through me. She slides her hands around my waist. Fireworks erupt the second she touches me, like she lit the fuse on a stick of dynamite.

"Fuck it." All self-control disappears into oblivion. I grab her cheeks with both my hands and slam my lips against hers.

She grips the sides of my T-shirt. The wall she formed encased her heart inside melt like butter. She swirls her tongue around mine, picking up the intensity.

My heart goes rogue, skipping beats and sending blood rushing through my veins. I pull away, taking a second to catch my breath. "You sure this is a good idea? Jesus Christ, what am I saying? Best idea ever.

She shakes her head. "I want you anyway."

Works for me. Sometimes the best adventures start with tequila and bad decisions. I flash a sexy half-smile and slide my hands down, grazing her breasts before making my way to her hand. I interlock my fingers with hers and take off toward the hotel room, dragging her with me.

She almost runs to keep up. What am I doing? It's like I need to get her in my room before she changes her mind. Dear God, don't let her overthink this whole deal. If she changes her mind now, I seriously might drop dead. It's amazing I'm not in cardiac arrest already.

We glide through the lobby, unnoticed by April, and sneak into the elevator right before the doors close. She moves closer, leaning on me as we ascend to floor ten. I grab her waist and press against her, showing her exactly how much I want her. She backs me up into the wall of the elevator and smacks her lips against mine, soft and first but more intense with every passing second. Holy hell, it's like a whole different Cora from a parallel universe came down to fill my deepest desires. Whatever the hell has gotten into her made her the perfect woman...well, for me anyway. Maybe I should take stock in tequila. My new favorite drink.

The elevator halts as soon as floor ten lights up. We walk out of the heavy doors the instant they open. Cora and I make a mad rush to room number 1018. I slide the key into the slot. Cora turns into a lustrous siren, pinning me against the door. She slithers her fingers down to the bottom of my t-shirt and slowly pulls the seam up, ripping the shirt off my head.

"Of course you have a perfect body." She feathers her fingers around my pecs, continuing down to my abs. A trail of tingles follow her soft touch. She keeps going following the outline of my abs and tracing the V that forms near the waist of my jeans.

Don't stop now, babe. You've got my stomach twisted into a million knots. I pull the key card out of my wallet. She takes it and reaches behind me, opening the door like a female MacGyver. I hook an arm around her waist and take three steps backwards, making sure we're both inside before kicking the door closed.

Moment of truth: alone in a hotel room, no distractions or interruptions, and no turning back. I bend down and scoop her up by her thighs, a move I've used since I dated Shelly Morgan back in high school. Cora instinctively wraps her legs around my waist and her arms my neck. Works like a charm, every time. She presses her lips against mine. I walk backwards towards the bed, knocking into a small table on my way.

She laughs and nuzzles into my neck. My pulse skyrockets. She goes for the neck every chance she gets. If she's a Goddamn vampire I deserve the bite. Why the hell do I feel like she's part of this whole deal? My Spidey sense needs a tune up.

I spin around and lower her onto the bed. Her laughter softens to a smile. I tuck a lock of fiery red hair behind her ear. The rest of the strands sprawl out along the bed, pulling me in the same way a flame does when I stare at it long enough.

"See something you like?" She nibbles her lip.

We're way past that. More like gazing at the sexiest woman in existence and want to devour every morsel. "You have no idea." I slam my lips to hers running my hand along the hourglass shape of her body. More curves than a roller coaster and just as exhilarating. I press against her hard, making sure she feels every inch of me.

I breathe so fast it's like I'm hyperventilating. Come on, Dex. Slow it down. It's not prom night and no one likes a three-second-Sam. I pull away, sending kisses down her neck to the seam of her halter top.

She lets out a soft moan when I run my tongue along the parts of her breast sticking out from the shirt. Might just be my favorite piece of woman's clothing. It's got to come off. I move one hand down to the bottom seam of the shirt and prop myself up with the other. She squirms when my fingers touch her hot skin. God, it's like she just stepped out of the flames of hell. Most women do.

She reaches down and pulls her shirt over her head. Jesus, straight-laced coroner turned nympho. Nice. I sit up and pull at the button of her jeans until it gives. Sliding a hand on each side, I rip down the painted-on denim and peel it to her toes. She arches her back to help with the journey. Black lace panties stick to her smoldering skin. Dear God, do all coroners wear fuck-me lingerie, or was she hoping to get lucky tonight? Who the hell cares?

I pounce on her in a split-second flat. She digs her fingers into my back, more like she's bracing herself for what's to come. It's going to be her, all night long. I slip a finger on each of her bra straps and slide them down her shoulders. She breathes faster. I kiss her skin, tracing the movements of my fingers. I circle a nipple with my calloused thumb and then follow the path with my tongue. She moans, weaving her fingers in my hair.

I summon my inner Fonzie and slide a hand up her back, unhooking her bra with a snap of my fingers and tossing it to the side. A burst of that sweet scent I'll remember until my dying day flows through the air. It sends me into a frenzy, like a shark when it smells blood. No more wasting time, I want her and I need her now.

I glide my nose along her ribs and down her flat stomach. The animal inside me flies to the surface, like a werewolf in the midst of a full moon. I grip the top of her panties with my teeth and pull down, paying special attention to her nether regions on my way.

"Dex..." Her voice sounds more like a plea than the way it should in the heat of passion.

Son of a bitch, she's bailing. "Uh-huh." I slither my hands down her thighs and continue.

"Never mind." She arches her back, helping me in my journey.

Goddammit. Why do chicks do that? Those two words should be taken out of the dictionary. Or it should be illegal to say them when you have more than two-thirds of your clothes removed. "You sure?"

"Oh yeah." She kicks off her panties and slides up higher on the bed.

"Back in the game." I rip off my jeans and boxers so fast they'll probably never untangle.

She makes the come-here gesture with her pointer finger. I hop on the bed like a bullfrog on steroids. She pulls me into a kiss, gliding her tongue around mine in an array of twists and turns. Within seconds I'm harder than marble. I press against her, trying to ease my way inside.

She jumps back. "Whoa, cowboy. Need to lasso that up first."

Huh, oh right. Where the hell is my wallet? I turn to find my jeans and see my wallet lying on the bottom of the bed. Divine intervention is on my side. I take out a condom and hold it with my teeth.

She pulls the side of the wrapper, ripping it down the middle. The sexy-as-fuck move sends electric shocks through me. I grab the condom and slide it on in two seconds flat. Now where were we? I lean down and kiss her, pressing myself against her at the same time. She flinches for a second. Okay, she's not into the rough sex, at least not yet. Start out slow and see what happens. I push slow and steady. She lets out a loud moan as her body takes me in. My heart thumps in my chest. She squeezes every inch of me, firing off nerve cells I didn't even know I had. Her tight body grabs onto me, like a sensual stranglehold.

I resist the urge to explode. Not yet, I need her to feel as good as I do right now. I thrust forward, slow at first increasing my passion. She matches my moves, digging her fingers deeper into my back. "Dex..."

The sound of her voice saying my name drives me to the brink of insanity. "Oh, Cora...do you feel that?" I slam into her hard.

She lets out a loud moan in between gasping for breaths. "Don't stop," she pleads. I grab her hips and pull her onto me. She squirms, trying to get away but I hold her tight. Nails rip down the skin of my back. "Oh God," she yells so loud I might have to send a bottle of champagne to the person staying next to us. Her muscles tense as she releases her built-up passion.

I lock my eyes onto her face, watching the euphoria flow through her body. "Come for me, baby." I thrust fast and hard, giving her all the pleasure possible. She wraps her legs around me like a python sucking up every morsel of ecstasy. I sink deep inside her, throbbing against the walls of her body. Fireworks ignite inside me. I grip the bedsheet and explode, muttering words I can't even decipher. I collapse on top of her and bury my face into her shoulder. We lie there, catching our breaths. I take in the sweet scent that seemed to magnify times a thousand.

Most definitely the best sexual experience of my life, the hundreds before her can't even remotely compare. Maybe I'll keep that factoid to myself. I slowly ease out of her and roll to the side. She lies there staring at the ceiling like she's just seen the second coming of Christ.

I know that what-the-fuck did I just do look gracing her face. Seen it more times than I can count, never cared until now. She's about the bail and I can't let that happen. I need her and not just for one night.

8

POINT OF NO RETURN

"Best first date ever." I prop myself on an elbow, tracing my fingers along the tattoo on the side of her ribs.

She gasps, pulling herself out of the trance. "Not a date." She springs into a sitting position.

"Okay then, best non-date ever." I roll over onto my back. Pain shoots through me like I just laid on a bed of nails. "Aww." I sit up, trying to blow it off and not look like a little girl. Pretty much feels like alcohol and salt poured into a gunshot wound.

She whips around and inspects my skin, running a finger alongside the path of the stinging. "I'm so sorry." She rests her forehead on my shoulder. "I knew this was a bad idea."

I turn toward around facing her and lift her chin. "I'm taking it as a compliment." I press my lips against hers, kissing her softly. "Be right back." I push the sheet aside and rise from the bed. My back aches with every move of my muscles. I need to at least splash some water on this before I run screaming through the halls. "Don't move."

"Any chance I can borrow a T-shirt?" She drapes the sheet over her body.

"You'll love this." I flinch as I open the drawer of the hotel's triple dresser and toss her my KISS shirt. Bet she thought I was trying to get in her pants when I told her I was a fan, which was also the case.

"You are full of surprises, Dex Jagger." She tosses on the two sizes too big T-shirt.

I stare at the black fabric, watching it caress her skin and for a split second I forget about the excruciating pain in my back. "Ditto." I take a step and fire burns through my skin. I pivot and walk to the bathroom, trying to suppress the urge to run and jump into a cold shower.

I close the door behind me and cover my mouth with my hand, letting out a muted groan. Okay, time to assess the damage. I turn toward the mirror and look over a shoulder. Holy fuck. It's like I pissed off Wolverine. Four long claw marks stretch across my back from the shoulder to the waist. I mean, I've driven girls wild before but she takes being a tiger in the bedroom literally. I soak a washcloth in cold water and rub the wound. The cool droplets douse the flames. No time to act like a pussy and hide in the bathroom. She's on the verge of jetting and I can't let her go.

I dispose of the condom in the waste paper basket and run a hand through my just fucked hair. I glance into the mirror. Jesus, my skin glistens like a virgin on prom night that just had her cherry popped.

I walk back into the bedroom. Cora's completely dressed and sliding on her boots. "I gotta go."

Dammit, I'm losing her. "Didn't think you were a love-me and leave-me kinda girl." She'd rather die than be a player, at least that's the impression I get from the way busts my balls. I unravel my boxers and jeans from last night and slide them on.

Her eyes scan me from head to toe, fixating on my abs. Is she ready to go for round two? "Come on, Dex. We both know this was a...mistake."

I move forward, keeping my eyes locked on hers. "An amazing one." I stop in front of her and take her hand. "For the record nothing that involves being with you is a mistake."

She looks down at the floor, biting her lip to suppress the smile about to burst thorough. Why is she fighting this so bad? Doesn't she get it? We're pretty much the perfect couple.

"Let me take you to breakfast. You gotta eat." I tip her chin up and press my forehead against hers. "And I'm not ready to let you go...not yet."

She takes a deep breath slowly exhaling, like an eternal struggle is going down in her brain. "I don't know..."

"Come on, what's the matter. Afraid you might start to like me?"

She lets out a tiny laugh. "Never going to happen." She runs her fingers along the lines of my abs. "You really need to put on a shirt." She moves back like she just touched a hot stove.

I raise an eyebrow. "See something you like?"

She rolls her eyes. I dig in the drawer and pull out the first shirt my hand touches, keeping my eyes locked on Cora. God knows if she'll bolt out the door if I turn my back. How can I make her understand being with me isn't the worst thing in the world?

"Eggs and pancakes?" I reach down and grab my wallet which made its way to the floor near the nightstand.

"Dex, I can't eat here. It's a small town and I can't explain what went down last night." She takes a few more steps toward the door.

"Fair enough. Then where? You name the place." I get it; she doesn't want to tarnish her reputation. She's made a name for herself here in Bumblefuck.

She shrugs. "I'm not hungry and I have a ton of work to do. I'll see you later." She takes off toward the door.

I jump forward and grab her arm before she moves out of

reach. "Listen. One date, that's all I ask. Then if you never want to see me again I'm out of your hair once the case is over." I release my grip on her wrist and cup her cheek with my hand. "Don't you get it? Last night was...earthshattering. I mean, apocalypse-like end-of-the-world amazing. You know it too. We're made for each other. Just give me a chance to prove it to you."

She closes her eyes and scrunches her eyebrows, like my words are causing her physical pain. "Dex..." She opens her eyes and stares into my soul. I search her face waiting for an answer. "Okay. As long as you can make us invisible."

I stare at her for a minute in disbelief. Holy shit, she said yes. "No problem. Pick you up at eight?" I lean in and give her a soft peck on the lips.

She softly kisses me back and swings around, rushing out the door. A challenge, since I don't have my cloak of invisibility I've got to get creative. Let's see, I need a place where everyone from town will avoid that has an essence of romance. Holy shit, I got it. Cora will be mine sooner than she thinks.

"Your chariot awaits." I lean against the doorjamb the second Cora swings open the door, and hold out a bouquet of tiger lilies. Roses are too cliché and from the way she clawed my back, I kinda think she's got some wild cat in her.

She eyes me from head to toe and leans to the right, checking out the wheels I rented. "Muscle car. I heard guys who drive those are overcompensating for something." She smirks.

"Didn't hear you complaining last night, babe." I raise an eyebrow.

Her face turns a thousand shades of scarlet. Damn, she's about to freak out. Where the hell is the filter between my brain and my mouth? Okay, so she started it but I don't have to be the one to finish it.

"Kidding…Mustangs are fast, furious, and really cool."

I stand up straight and hand her the flowers like the gentleman she was expecting me to be tonight.

She takes the lilies and breathes in the sweet scent. "They're beautiful." She sets them on a table in her office. "Mustangs don't usually deter attention. Hard to be invisible with a 5.0 engine."

"Nice, a chick who knows her cars. One more thing that makes you amazing." Great save. "Trust me, it'll be like you used vanishing cream." I eye her office, looking toward the back wall. "Do you live here?"

She nods. "Yeah, I bought the building when I first moved here and live in the apartment upstairs. More than I need but I don't have to travel far too work." She steps outside and locks the door behind us.

I place my hand in the small of her back and guide her toward the candy apple red machine. I open the door for her. "My lady."

She chuckles, giving me a half eye roll and sits in the seat. I slowly close the door and jet to the other side. God knows if she'll change her mind and jump out. Hell, she might even do that if we're moving.

She clicks on her seatbelt and turns toward me. "Okay, I'm ready to be amazed."

A million derogatory comments flow through my mind but I manage to keep them to myself. "It's a surprise."

"I hate surprises." She fidgets with the radio until she finds the classic rock station. "Won't Get Fooled Again" blasts through the speakers.

I resist the urge to crank up the volume. "Maybe I can change that."

I turn the corner and pull onto a dirt road. April at the hotel can talk a dog off of a meat wagon. She gave me the scoop on the town's old logging roads that lead deep into the woods. Everyone's pretty much scared shitless to venture out hiking so we'll be invisible to the public, just like she asked. Okay, so an SUV would be the way to go but hell, it's not as sexy as a Mustang.

"Are you planning on killing me and hiding the body?" She sweeps her eyes along the windshield, taking in the landscape of the thick forest. A smile graces her face.

Who's she kidding? She loves it out here. Quiet, isolated, everything she wants. "Nope, just want you all to myself. Plus, I might be able to catch you if you run off."

"Doubt it." She nibbles her lip. "You didn't want intel to solve the case back at the biker bar, you wanted to hit up the best places to go parking."

I take my hands off the steering wheel for a second and hold them up in the air. "Caught me."

She laughs.

We pull up to a clearing through the thick trees. For once, I planned ahead. An oversized flannel blanket spreads across the soft grass lined with candles along the perimeter. Two wineglasses stick out of a straw picnic basket in the middle of the blanket along with a bottle of Moscato chilling in an ice filled silver bucket.

"You did all this for me?" She opens the car door and rushes toward the set-up before I have a chance to run to the passenger door and hold it open for her. She covers her mouth with her hands.

I point to the treetops covering the area with a canopy of leaves. "You wanted invisible."

She drops her hands and turns toward me. She struggles to turn the smile beaming from her face to a smirk. "You know you could've burnt down the whole forest, right?"

I shake my head. "Give me some credit." I grab one of the candles and hold it up to her. "Look...flameless."

She nibbles her lip and nods. "Okay, I guess I like some surprises."

"I've got a few more up my sleeve." I sling an arm around her shoulder and guide her to the blanket. For once, she doesn't flinch. Either she's starting to like me or has gotten used to my antics.

"I expect nothing less." She kneels onto the soft fabric next to the picnic basket.

I follow suit, facing her. She shifts her gaze, looking around the crisp leaves like it's the first time she's ever been in the woods.

"See something you like?" I wink. My eyes gravitate like magnets to her red strands blowing in the soft breeze. Her porcelain skin glistens off the cool moonlight casting sparkles along her purple sundress. Closest I've ever seen to an angel on earth.

She grabs a napkin from the picnic basket and tosses it at me, pulling me out of my trance. "Do you?"

"Oh yeah!" It slips out of my mouth before I have a chance to silence my inner cave-man voice.

"Are you about to snap into a Slim Jim or something?" She tips her head and gives me that you've-got-to-be-kidding me look.

"Or something...I wasn't finished. What I meant was that nothing in the world matches your beauty, and I can't believe I'm lucky enough to be sitting here with you." Nice save, Dex.

Her cheeks flush brighter than the reddest rose. "Might be the best compliment of my life."

"I'm just getting started." I open the picnic basket and set two plates out along with the wineglasses. I take out a container filled with cheese and crackers, one with grapes, and one containing ham and cheese sliders, turkey sliders, and peanut butter and jelly sliders. "Only thing I've seen you eat is a lime with your tequila."

She slaps me playfully and grabs the bag of chocolate covered pretzels I brought for dessert. "First thing you need to know, I'm not one of those girls who don't eat." She shoves two pretzels in her mouth. They disappear like they've been beamed up by aliens. "Second, I pretty much like everything, and third... this is the best date I've been on in years."

I pop open the wine and fill both our glasses. I hold mine up. "To kindred souls who are meant to be."

She lifts her glass and clinks it with mine, downing a huge sip. "Sounds like a famous quote."

I put my hand on my heart. "Made it up about ten seconds ago."

"Maybe you're meant for more than hunting monsters." She grabs a turkey sandwich and takes a bite.

"Yeah, maybe I'm meant to be with you." Okay, so I'm coming on a little strong but I can't help it. Everything about her pulls me into a vortex of passion. I float around unable to resist the gravitational force she has on me. I've already gotten in her pants and the second she leaves my field of vision, I can't wait to see her again. I've heard tales of people falling under a woman's spell, but I figured they were weak and it was all bullshit. How the hell did it happen to me?

She flashes a smile but doesn't say a word. She slugs her wine and pops a grape into her mouth. "I know nothing about you."

I scrunch my eyebrows. "More than most." I shrug. "Shoot, what do you want to know?"

"Where's home?" She searches my face like a human lie detector.

I've got nothing to hide from her. She already knows my

deepest secret. It's not like you can tell a chick you hunt supernatural beasts, although it's probably a pretty good pick up line. "Right now it's here."

She sighs. Dammit, I'm losing her already. Jesus Christ, no wonder people say relationships are hard. Of course, this is probably the closest I've ever come to one.

"Small town in Pennsylvania. Trees as far as the eye can see. You'd love it." I stuff a ham and cheese sandwich in my mouth and finish it one gulp. "My turn."

"Okay, but I still have the right to plead the fifth." She licks some melted chocolate off of her top lip.

My heart goes into overdrive, beating like I've snorted meth. I squirm and adjust my positon trying to conceal the beast she's invoking. "You know mysterious girls are so damn sexy."

"Same goes for guys, especially ones driving Mustangs." She finishes the rest of the wine in her glass.

I pour us each some more. "How about that tattoo, what's it mean?"

"Most people never see it." She nibbles on some cheese. "It's Japanese for fox."

"Foxy lady...nice." I raise my eyebrows and sport a half-smile half-smirk.

"Something like that." She tears through the rest of the pretzels.

Note to self: *next time bring more chocolate.* "So, are you convinced?"

"Uh, that you're sweet, thoughtful, and not the jerk I pegged you for?" She taps her fingers on her glass. "Eh, getting there."

"About the we-belong-together part?" I fidget with my fingers. Moment of truth, if she says she wants nothing to do with me I have to accept it, end of story.

She shrugs. "You forgot one important thing."

What the hell is she talking about? For once, I planned. Got food, wine, dessert, made us invisible, brought romance. What gives? "Not a chance."

She nods. "Kick-ass music."

Would it be inappropriate to propose right now? I breathe deep and take in her sweet scent. Hotter than an angel, brains like Einstein, a body that can bring the devil to his knees, amazing taste in music, who wouldn't want to spend forever with the only perfect woman on the planet?

"I'm on it, babe." I dash over to the Mustang and flip the key to turn on the radio. I've already preset the classic rock channel. "Forever" by KISS blasts through the speakers. I look to the sky for a brief minute. Thank you to the divine intervention that made this happen.

I walk over to Cora and hold out my hand. "They're playing our tune. Can't let down the KISS Army."

She looks down at the blanket and taps her fingers on her legs. Why is everything such a struggle? It's not like we're in the middle of the Footloose movie. She shifts her gaze toward me and slides her hand in mine.

I lift it and her body follows. Her fingers tremble like it's the dance of death. She already knows my moves, not sure why she's so shy all of a sudden. I entwine my fingers with hers and pull her close. The scarlet strands of her hair whisk by me the same way coral did in my friend's fish tank. Alive and graceful, floating through the air without a care in the world. A few strands caress my face, sending tingles along my skin. I wrap my arms around her waist and move closer, until the heat of my body radiates through her.

Her heart vibrates in her chest so loud I can feel it. I press my cheek against hers and sway to the music. The friction between us electrifies me. I adjust my stance to prevent the bulge in my pants from scaring her into the next county. She ignores my moves and comes closer. Is she making a move?

Maybe the sexy siren is rearing its head. Never thought I'd be lucky enough to have that happen twice in one lifetime. Only one way to find out.

I slide my cheek down until our lips are barely touching. She sucks in a deep breath. It's just me and Cora, the rest of the world disappeared. Tonight I want to take my time, savor every morsel of her being. I graze my bottom lip along hers, soft at first and then growing in intensity. She holds my hand tighter. I slide my tongue around hers twisting and turning into a spiral of passion.

She lets out a soft moan and releases her death grip on my hand, tracing the hairline at my neck. Chills sweep through me as she weaves her fingers in my hair, skimming my skin with her fingernails. The feeling invigorates every nerve in my body. Every ounce of my being wants to throw her down on the blanket and fuck her into next week but I need to relish in every second I have with her. Plus, she's not some chick whose name I won't remember three days from now. She's the only woman I've ever wanted to spend more than a night with, and it scares the shit out of me.

I move my hands to her waist and guide her down toward the blanket. Her arms tremble. Wait, that's me shaking like some teenybopper that just saw the movie "Halloween" for the first time. Did she put some kind of voodoo curse on me? I breathe deep trying to kick my body back into its former glory. Why the hell would I be nervous about fucking Cora? I mean, been there done that, sure as hell would buy the t-shirt if they had one. My heart beats into overdrive sending adrenaline through my body. I get it, she's sober and I'm about to do something I've never done before…make love instead of fucking.

Come on, Dex don't be a pussy. Pull yourself together. I send soft kisses down her neck, sliding my nose along their path. She breathes so fast she's almost panting. I slide my hand over her breast to the length of her dress, touching her thigh right under the hem line.

She parts her legs like she's flashing a neon sign saying *Enter Here*. I feather my fingers along her inner thigh, moving to her nether regions. Her soft skin feels like smooth porcelain and looks just as flawless. She squirms and moves closer as I run my thumb over her panties. Oh yeah, she wants me just as bad. Maybe I'll give her a little taste of what's to come. I grip the string of her bikini panties with each hand and slowly slide them off. She arches her back to help me in the journey. I glide them down her legs and navigate around her black high heels until I throw them God knows where. I softly kiss her knee, and continue up to her thigh. She moans, moving the blanket like a Mexican jumping bean. All about anticipation, babe. I shoot my kisses up her inner thigh until I reach my goal. Many girls have told me I know my way around a woman. No sense in letting a gift go to waste.

I slide my tongue around her most sensual areas, circling it and sucking just enough to send her shooting to the starts. She lets out an erotic cry and grabs my head with both hands, pushing me harder against her.

The claws come out, literally. I grab both her wrists and pin them to the blanket, pressing every inch of myself against her. I want her…now. I release my grip and she moves her hands down to my gray T-shirt, ripping it off over my head. I tug at the button of my jeans like someone threw acid on them and it was burning through my skin. Pretty much feels the same way. It finally gives. I take out my wallet and sift through it with one hand, grabbing the condom I put in there just in case things went how I wanted them to tonight.

Her light brown eyes, filled with lustful passion, lock with mine. "Dex, I need you."

"Never have to ask me twice." I kick off my jeans and boxers in a move I should have patented, and rip open the condom wrapper, sliding it on in warp speed. "Oh baby, you never have to wait...ever." I slam into her, hard and deep.

She lets out a loud moan, like the ones you hear in a porno flick. "Oh, God."

No baby, God has nothing to do with this. It's all me. I thrust hard and steady, growing even more with every move. Not sure if it's the woods or the way she makes me feel. She turns me into a beast, one that needs to satisfy her cravings and mine.

She leans back, matching my moves and pressing her fingers against my skin. Passion builds inside creating a firestorm. I can barely hold on. She wraps her legs around me into a stranglehold and pushes me deep inside her. I roll to the side and move to a sitting position, gripping Cora's back. I need to see her face, to watch her body overcome with pleasure.

I grab onto her hips and guide her, slamming her onto me. Her eyes lock onto mine. Jesus it's like they're glowing. Must be the moonlight, or I can do a hell of a lot more to a woman than I thought. Her eyebrows lower and her face flushes. She digs into my back and opens her mouth as she moans. Holy hell, not a prettier sight in the world. She grinds back and forth, dripping onto my legs. I stare into her eyes. They slightly close, almost like they're begging me to keep going. Oh yeah, babe. Don't forget who makes you come like that. I try to hold out longer but the way she moves against my body sends me into another world. I explode inside of her, letting the love and passion flow between us.

No dirty talk this time. Nah, tonight's special, not some cheap after a few drinks kind of night. I want her to remember our first official date as one of the best in her life on all levels.

I bury my head in her shoulder and we take a few seconds to catch our breaths. "Best first date ever," I say in between gasps.

She playfully hits my shoulder. "I'd say it's like our tenth date."

I lean back and stare at her face, flushed with passion yet completely flawless. "Hmm, you made it clear all the other times we've been together is work related. Nope, this is our first official date."

She bites her lip, holding in a smile and rolls her eyes. "Whatever, best date I've been on in…I don't know how long."

"Told you, one date and you'll be convinced we belong together."

"I didn't say that." She eases off of me and sits back onto the blanket.

I ball her panties in my palm and hand them to her. "Why are you making this so hard?" I slide on my boxers and jeans, and sit Indian style on the blanket. Typically, we should be lying and cuddling but nothing between Cora and I is normal.

"Dex, let's just enjoy the night." She slips on her panties and leans against my chest.

"Chicks are impossible to figure out." I let out a deep breath and wrap my arms around her. The sweet scent along with the musty forest sends me into another dimension.

"Is this news to you?" She turns her head toward me and snickers.

"You're not like other girls, guess it just took me by surprise." Okay, so girls never make it this hard on me. If she didn't like me she sure as hell wouldn't be here. So, what's the problem?

She breathes deep and slowly exhales, running her finger along my forearm. "It's been a long time, can't we just take it slow?"

I rest my head on her shoulder and nibble her neck. "Fair enough."

"Plus, I can't think straight until you put on a shirt." She lets out a chuckle.

"I'll be bare chested forever." I pull us down onto the blanket and hover above her.

"No complaints here."

I lean down to kiss her. A split second later, I'm flying across the meadow. My back slams against a tree. Pain radiates from my neck to my tailbone, adding insult to my clawed up back. What the hell just happened?

I lift my weary eyes and stare into a red abyss. Dark shoulder-length hair, about the right age, holy shit. A low growl erupts in his throat echoing through the forest.

Oh my God. "Cora!" I yell but it sounds like a whisper. The wind is knocked out of my lungs from the impact. I scan the woods and focus my gaze back to the vamp. Dear God, please let her live.

9
REVELATIONS

My chest tightens, strangling my heart from a million directions. Where the hell is she? A pit forms in my stomach. I glance at the treetops praying she's not hanging from any of them. Whatever happens to her is my fault, one hundred percent. I was supposed to protect her and I drag her out here in the middle of nowhere knowing there's a vamp on the loose. Why the fuck am I so stupid? Guess I was thinking with my dick again.

Trees rustle in the depths of the forest. The vamp spins around to check it out. Adrenaline flows through my body so fast my hands shake. I pounce into action and hightail it to the car, leaping into the backseat. I rip open my duffle bag and grab a syringe filled with dead man's blood, a silver chain, and my gun.

He rips off the back door and stands in front of me, showing me his fangs. I lean back in the seat and point my pistol at him, holding it with both hands. He licks his lips like he's about to bite into a juicy steak. No need to get too antsy, not happening tonight.

He laughs, showing his fangs. "Guns won't hurt me."

I shoot two rounds into his chest. "They do if they're loaded with silver bullets."

He flies through the air like the hand of God pushed him and knocks into a huge tree trunk. I've only got about ten seconds so I need to use them wisely. I spring into action like a gazelle and wrap the silver chain around him, tying him to the tree. He struggle to break free but the chain burns his skin, sending smoke trails through the air. Time to talk. Or die.

His skin sizzles against the metal, melting through his skin. A primal scream flows from his mouth, echoing through the dark night. He closes his eyes and leans his head against the tree.

I hold the syringe filled with Dead Man's Blood in the air. "Spill it. What are you doing in Whispering Pines?"

He eyes the needle. "Like it matters, I'm dead anyway."

I step on the chain, digging it deeper into his fresh wounds. "Yeah, since the moment you were bit. Why the hell are you here?"

He sucks in a few breaths, lulling the pain. "Cyrus...the master of our nest and our maker." He struggles a bit, and then relaxes his muscles. "Some girl or something posing as one killed his mate here." He chuckles and turns his red eyes toward me. "I got pulled over for speeding here once. The genius sheriff missed the blood dripping from my trunk. Idiot. When Cyrus put out the call to avenge Lizzie's death, I jumped at the chance. Figured it be quick and easy."

I nod. "Yeah, I dealt with the sheriff, too." Jesus, why am I acting like this vamp is suddenly my BFF? Time to get some answers. I pace around the front of the tree, watching the vamp's every move. "So Wonder Woman took out the head vamp's chick. Any clue who she is?"

If there was another hunter on the case, I sure as hell

would've run into her. I mean, she'd have to deal with local law enforcement and with Cora. Jesus, where the hell is Cora? Maybe this bloodsucker brought friends.

He shakes his head. "All I know is, Lizzie had a pile of red hair balled up in her hand and her throat was slashed as if Freddy Kruger got a hold of her." He tips his chin toward me and locks eyes with mine, like he's reaching into my soul and about to rip it out. "Even Ruby didn't know what could do that to a 300 year old vampire."

A wave of dizziness flows through sending a chill down to my toes. "What did you say?"

He smiles, blood covering his teeth.

That son of a bitch! I spring into action and grab him by the throat, pushing the silver chain hard against his skin. "Where's Ruby?" I press the needle of the syringe to his neck, holding the plunger. He flashes a sly smile.

A split second later, I'm flying through the air like a tornado whisked me into oblivion. My back slams a tree trunk. What the hell just happened? No way that vamp got out of the chain. I open my eyes, slowly focusing on the dark figure in front of me. Oh shit, I'm screwed.

A Vin Diesel lookalike pushes my chest, holding me against the tree with one arm. "Where is it?"

He must be Cyrus. I gasp, trying to suck in a few shallow breaths. Guess the bastard knocked the wind out of me. "What?" My voice cracks.

"The kitsune. You were just with her," he mutters through gritted teeth.

"What the hell are you talking about? I was on a date that you vamps crashed…and where's my sister?"

He pushes me against the tree harder, knocking my head off the dry bark. "I'm asking the questions here."

A red blur invades my field of vision. The vamp releases his grip. I slide down the tree until my ass hits the ground. I stare straight ahead trying to focus. Everything spins. Did the son of a bitch bite me? I slap my hands along my neck, going into full panic mode. Okay, I'm clean. Pain radiates along the back of my head. Where is the bastard?

Leaves rustle to my right. I spring to my feet and follow the ruckus. Trees snap from their trunks as if an invisible cyclone sweeps the area. Last time I saw anything like this was in The Wizard of Oz. Somehow I doubt a house is going to fall on the bloodsucker. Oh shit, there're two of them. I gaze around, sweeping the forest and trying to get my bearings straight. The other vamp has to be tied to the tree. Silver burns Cyrus just as quick so he couldn't have freed him. If I can take out one vamp I have a better chance.

A lump lies along the ground. I rush toward it, ducking to avoid the debris flying in the air. The silver chain couldn't have killed him that fast. I reach the vamp and push his limp body with my foot, rolling him to the side. Blood drips down his arm to his fingertip. I stare at what used to be his throat, ripped to shreds like a T-rex swiped his claws across it.

My heart goes into overdrive, beating fast and furious. What the hell else is out here? Chills sweep through me. I've got to find Cora before anything else does. I pull my gun out from the back of jeans. I guess it's a miracle it's still there and in one piece. Colt makes one hell of a firearm. I shift my focus toward the commotion and run straight for it holding the pistol out in front of me with both hands.

Blurs of red and black zip from side to side like I'm watching a movie in supersonic speed. I aim right in front of the black blur, hoping for a direct hit. Slow and steady I press the trigger, sending an immense pop resonating through the air. Dammit, a miss. I refocus and think back to the time I got a full spray of mace right in the eye when I was hunting a werewolf a few years ago. All I could see were brown streaks of fur. Come on Dex, focus. I squint, staring straight ahead and press my finger against the trigger. My heart pounds in my ears. The shot fires, hitting the black blur a split second before it leaves my field of vison.

A loud moan fills the air. The blur slows enough to allow my eyes to take in the figure. Holy shit, it's the vamp. He drops to his knees holding his throat. Blood seeps between the spaces of his fingers. He looks at me and then stares up at the sky. He falls forward and drops to the ground.

I stand tall, my eyes stick to him like glue. What the hell just happened? My arms tremble. I pivot from side to side sweeping the forest line, gun still held out in front of me. A figure creeps forward.

I focus on its golden yellow eyes with narrow pupils shining at me like the sun. Blood drips from its razor sharp claws. I breathe fast and heavy, about to hyperventilate. My heartbeat races into a frenzy. I shift my focus to a mop of red hair. A breeze blows though, sending the sweet smell I'd know anywhere in my direction. I gasp, "Cora?"

She locks eyes with me, and drops to her knees. She's surrendering even though she can rip me to shreds in a second. My body shakes like I'm standing in Antarctica. This can't be happening. I must've hit my head so hard against that tree I'm hallucinating.

She looks to the ground and then lifts her chin, staring down the barrel of my Colt. I hold the grip tight out in front of me, trying to steady my trembling arms. Jesus Christ, I can't do it. She's not a monster. She can't be.

I lower my arms and pace in a small circle. Gut-wrenching pain flows through my chest keeping a death grip on my heart. I wince and lower my gaze. A split second later I raise my arms and point the gun straight at her. She lied to me, been doing it this whole time. Was I next on her termination list?

"Just do it." She hangs her head as if she's been exiled.

I squint for a second and shake my head. "I can't."

Cora's not some bloodsucker or shape-shifter. For Christ's sake she just killed two vamps. She could've done me in any time she wanted, but hell, I'm still here.

"Why?" Her body goes back to its original form, pure perfection.

Is she for real? Maybe because I haven't stopped thinking about her since the second we met. For the first time in my life, I want to stay in this one-horse town that has nothing to offer except a greasy diner food and an idiot sheriff, just so I can be with her. She makes me want to be the person I never thought I could. "The world is a better place with you in it."

What the hell am I saying? She's not human. Every ounce of my being needs to get rid of anything and everything with unnatural powers.

She moves forward faster than a gazelle and presses the barrel of the gun against her chest. "We both know you don't believe that." She closes her eyes and breathes deep.

Is she insane? Why the hell does she want to die? Does a Kitsune, or whatever the hell she is, have a lower value on life than the rest of us? She's right though, I should kill her, but I can't.

"I don't know what I believe anymore, Cora." I toss my gun into a patch of high grass. The last five minutes turned everything to shit. I run both hands through my hair. Come on, Dex, pull it together. Nothing new, just life throwing another one of its fucking curve balls at you.

She leans back on her heels, searching my face. "I'm sorry." It comes out as a whisper.

Yeah, me too. Sorry I crashed here, that I stayed, and that I fell I love with someone I should destroy. Son of a bitch, maybe it runs in the family. Cora's nothing like a bloodsucker but I get what happened to Ruby—well sort of. Goddammit I know better than to hook up with a chick for more than one night. Nothing but problems, bigger than I ever imagined. I've got to get out of here. I pull myself to my feet and trudge to the car, resisting the urge to look back at the most beautiful sight ever to lay my eyes upon. I slide into the driver's seat and fire up the engine. A quick stop at the sheriff's office tomorrow and I'll look at Whispering Pine's in my rearview mirror. No matter what I have to leave behind.

KITSUNE: *a very rare creature that appears to look human but can shapeshift, similar to a werewolf but more foxlike. Primary weapon is their claws. When attacking their pupils turn yellow and narrow. They possess super speed and strength, and emit a floral odor that appeals to humans, calming them and producing a euphoric effect. Their hair captures glints of sunlight that helps increase their power. They feed on human brain matter, and without it they will die. Kitsunes can be killed by stabbing them in the heart with a silver dagger or a silver bullet.*

I run my fingers along the screen of my cell phone. Google, where the hell would I be without you? No wonder I've never heard of a kitsune, I can probably find a unicorn faster. So she eats brains. Guess my picnic food was an all-out fail. I get it; she survives from eating the stiff's brains in the morgue, except for some vampire delicacies. Even though she's not human, she's not a monster.

I shove the phone in my back pocket and head into the sheriff's office. Sheriff Townsend sits back in his chair with his feet on the desk. His hat covers his eyes. I shake my head, working hard as usual. I step inside and slam the door.

Sheriff Townsend jumps out of his chair. "Dex, umm, can I help you?" He breathes hard and heavy, like he's just seen a ghost.

I roll my eyes...moron. "Just stopping by to tell you I caught the villain. You were right all along...animal attack. I went up to take another look, found a mountain lion. It almost shredded my back."

He sports an ear-to-ear grin and nods his head. "I know what goes on in my town. Where is it now?"

I ball my hands into fists. Relax, Dex, you need to convince this idiot everything's fine and get the hell out of here. "I shot him in the chest. He stumbled off and I couldn't find him, probably in some cave. No way he survived. Anyway, investigation is over. I'm heading out." I walk up to him and hold out my hand. "Great working with you, sheriff. Take care."

He shakes my hand. "You too, Dex."

I turn and walk out the door. Worst acting I've ever seen on both our parts. We'd definitely win one of those Golden Raspberry Awards. Doesn't matter, nothing changed. Now that this mess is over I need to refocus and find Ruby.

I step outside and shut the door behind me. The warm breeze rustles the leaves. I close my eyes and take a deep breath. The aroma of sweet nectar flows through my soul. I gasp and pop open my eyes.

Cora stands at the bottom of the steps. She locks eyes with me and jumps back like I'm about to end her right now in front of the sheriff's office. Come on, she knows me better than that.

I hold out my hands. "Do you really think I'd hurt you?"

She swallows hard and shrugs. "You hate me right now." She sighs. "I didn't want any of it to happen. I told you this was a bad idea from the beginning but you wouldn't listen and I...I couldn't stay away from you." Her whole body trembles.

I walk down the steps and face her. The sweet smell that I could make millions if I market flows through the air, wrapping around me like octopus tentacles. My heart pounds faster with every second. "I don't hate you," I whisper.

She looks up at me, her golden eyes staring into the depths of my being. "You should. I lied to you. Letting you believe I'm something I'm not is pretty much the same thing."

I shake my head. "I would've killed you if you told me before but now..." I take a deep breath and slowly exhale. "I know what you are, what you do, how you live." I tip her chin up and take a step closer. "I don't care about any of it." I press my forehead against hers. "Cora, I'm in love with you and nothing else matters." I press my lips to hers, putting all the passion I feel for her into this one kiss.

She relaxes her muscles and slowly pulls away. "Of all the guys in the world, I had to fall in love with a hunter." She smiles.

I gesture behind me. "The choices in this town weren't too great."

She laughs. "So what happens now? You know this is crazy, right?"

I snicker. "You know I like to live on the wild side, babe."

"Don't call me babe." She playfully smacks my arm.

"Why, you going to do, kick my ass? I might like it." I raise my eyebrows.

"Just because you can google doesn't mean you know everything about me."

"I can't wait to find out more." I wrap my arms around her waist, pulling her close against me. "I finally got a lead on Ruby. I've got to try to find her." I tuck a loose strand of her fiery hair behind an ear. "You know, I could use a kick-ass kitsune to help me take down the nest. Ever try your hand at hunting?"

She shakes her head. "I don't know...I like to keep to myself and stay under the radar."

I press my lips together and nod. Yeah, she doesn't need to get herself involved in all of this. It's my fight, not hers.

"But I know where she is, one of the perks of eating vamp brains." She wraps her arms around my neck. "I could show you and we can see what happens." She holds out my Colt and hands it to me.

Oh my God, my baby. I was planning on searching the woods for her before I left. I take it and stick it in the back of my jeans. I break into a cheek-to-cheek smile. "Ready for a road trip?"

"Only if I get to pick the music." She winks.

I grab her hand and pull her toward my Harley. "Just got a new radio installed complete with helmet speakers."

"Any way I can talk you into taking my car?" She nibbles her lip.

I stare at her teeth catching the pink flesh. "Maybe I can be persuaded." I hand her a helmet. "Let's get you packed."

She takes the helmet. "I can't believe I'm doing this." She slides it on over her red hair.

"Just wait and see all the trouble we can get into." I slip on the helmet and mount the bike. She jumps on the back and wraps her arms around me. I play side one of KISS's Destroyer through the speakers. "We're about to embark on a wild ride. Hold on tight, babe. We're just getting started."

THE END

Check out the series that started it all, Blissful Tragedy and Blissful Disaster are now available.

www.authoramygale.com

Sign up for the Gale Gazette and be the first to know about exclusive contests, new releases, and upcoming events.
http://www.authoramygale.com/newsletter.html

ABOUT THE AUTHOR

USA Today bestselling author **Amy L Gale** is a romance author by night, pharmacist by day who loves rock music and the feel of sand between her toes. She's the author of USA Today Bestseller, Resisting Darkness, Amazon New Adult Bestsellers, *Blissful Tragedy and Blissful Valentine,* along with *Christmas Blitz,* and *Blissful Disaster*. When she's not writing, she enjoys baking, scary movies, rock concerts, and reading books at the beach. She lives in the lush forest of Northeastern Pennsylvania with her husband, seven cats, and golden retriever, Sadie. You can find her at:

www.authoramygale.com

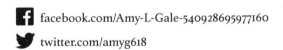

facebook.com/Amy-L-Gale-540928695977160

twitter.com/amyg618

Read More from Amy L. Gale

www.authoramygale.com

Made in the USA
Middletown, DE
22 July 2025

11095388R00071